THE LIST BOOKS
~ 3 ~

The Paper List

By
Dianne J. Wilson

THE PAPER LIST

A List Book Romance

Order, Chaos, and the

Grace In-between

Book 3

Copyright © 2022 by Dianne J. Wilson

This book is a work of fiction set in a fictional location. Any reference to historical or contemporary figures, places, or events, whether fictional or actual, is a fictional representation. Any resemblance to actual persons living or dead is entirely coincidental.

All rights reserved. No portion of this book may be reproduced in any form without written permission from the author except in the case of brief quotations embodied in critical articles or reviews.

eBook editions are licensed for your personal enjoyment only. eBooks may not be re-sold, copied, or given away to other people. If you would like to share an eBook edition, please purchase an additional copy for each person you share it with.

Contact information:

dianne@diannejwilson.com

Scripture quotations from The Authorized (King James) Version. Rights in the Authorized Version in the United Kingdom are vested in the Crown. Reproduced by permission of the Crown's patentee, Cambridge University Press

All Scripture quotations, unless otherwise indicated, are taken from the Holy Bible, New International Version®, NIV®. Copyright ©1973, 1978, 1984, 2011 by Biblica, Inc.™ Used by permission of Zondervan. All rights reserved worldwide. www.zondervan.com The "NIV" and "New International Version" are trademarks registered in the United States Patent and Trademark Office by Biblica, Inc.™

Cover Art by Dianne J. Wilson

Cover Image ID - shutterstock_594 031730

Feather Logo © designed by Hayley Wilson

DIANNE J. WILSON

Emile,

*ENTJ education
plotting & konkeling
teachats about not giving up*

~ thank you ~

You are Heaven's best gift to our family.

*Now faith is the substance of things hoped for,
the evidence of things not seen.*

Hebrews 11 v 1 (kjv)

To You, Dear Reader

Paper-making involves ripping, soaking, sifting, and sponging, followed by a lengthy drying time. It is a tedious, crazy process that requires a lot of effort and patience. Honestly?
It's tempting to call it a mess, not a masterpiece.
Life might feel like that for you - all ripped up, with odd shreds of this and that thrown in, sopping wet and uncomfortable. Sometimes you may find a crunched up, dried out, petal and wonder ... why is this in here?
A mess or a masterpiece? The difference is in the hands of the Artist. In God's hands, every tiny shard thrown into the mix of your life will contribute to beauty once He's done.
For now, be at peace, knowing ...
The One who holds you won't let go.
You are free to hope, free to dream.
Your story is being written and the Author is thoroughly smitten with you.
With love,

Chapter One

To Emma, weddings involved ripping. Lots and lots of ripping.

She sat at the enormous desk where she most liked to do her work, shredding paper and dumping the bits into a bowl of water to make the soggy mulch that would become the exquisite handmade paper she used for invitations. It was a tedious, slow process, but the results were worth it.

Ripping aside, weddings had always filled Emma with a strange sense of morbid fascination. The crazy pressure for everything to be *special* and *perfect* never failed to twist her stomach into a knot. Life seldom dished up *perfect* and starting a new life wrapped up in all that seemed like a setup for disappointment.

And yet here she was, running her own little business, *The Paper List*, priding herself on delighting the fussiest of brides.

She stirred in gold flakes and watched them drift between the bits of rose petals. Her petals were home-grown, harvested from the rose bushes in the garden and dried in the gentle sun on her porch, filtered through vine leaves.

Her part in the happily-ever-afters was small; one-of-a-kind invitations, individually handmade, with matching table markers and thank you cards. Emma had perfected the art of paper-making to ensure that all her brides got something unique, elegant, and breath-taking.

The wedding cards she made took a lot of effort, but she prayed as she worked, soaking the couple in blessings from Heaven. Sometimes she imagined herself sitting next to God and talking to Him about the bridal pair, finding out from Him what they'd need most and praying for those things.

Beyond that? The couple themselves had to make the rest of forever work. Once they'd paid her bill, she was done.

Regardless of her feelings about the drama of wedding days, her business had brought in enough to keep a roof over her head and food on the table.

She dipped the wooden-framed screen into the bowl where the paper mulch, gold flecks, and petals floated. A slow swirl helped ensure that the single piece she was working on had all the elements.

She hauled it out and upended it on the bamboo cloth, pressing out the excess water with a sponge. Perfect.

Only two hundred and ninety-nine to go.

This was the biggest order she'd received yet and it was going to stretch her to get it all done on time, but this job would cover her rental payment and she'd do it even if she didn't sleep for the next month.

The rental home she lived in was old, small, and perfect for her. Even down to the vast rose garden that supplied her with a steady stream of petals and the birds that woke her gently every morning. It wasn't her house, but it sure was her home.

Her phone rang and she dried off her hands to answer it. "The Paper List, Emma speaking."

"Am I speaking to Miss Redwood who is working on the Holmes wedding?" The voice on the other end was low and gravelly. Not Thomas, the bridegroom. He had a bit of a squeaky voice that she'd always thought was a little unfortunate.

"That's right. I'm working on those cards right now." A vague sense of unease brushed over her.

"Um, about that." The man cleared his throat. "I'm sorry to say, the wedding has been called off. Mr. Holmes won't need your services."

"I'm not sure I understand." Emma's rent amount flashed through her mind, followed by quick panic. There was no way she could cover it this late in the month without this wedding income.

"Mr. Holmes will pay ten percent as a cancellation fee."

Ten percent? Maybe her landlord would let her live in ten percent of the property. She could probably get used to living and running her business from the bathroom. Wait, no! What nonsense.

"I'm sorry but I don't even know who you are. How do I know that I can trust you?" Emma's senses were sharpened by adrenalin. "You might be a jilted ex with ulterior motives. For all I know, you could be trying to sabotage the happy couple."

"Miss Redwood, I can assure you that I am not the ex, I have no ulterior motives and they are currently, as of today, no longer a happy couple."

"That still doesn't answer my question. Who are you?" Emma was grabbing at straws and she knew it.

"Benedict Holmes, Thomas's older brother and best man."

Silence stretched as Emma scrambled for something to say.

Frustration boiled. "Obviously not a very good best man. If you were, you'd have been able to keep them on track through all the wedding stress and not let this disaster happen."

• • • • ● • ● • • •

Benedict Holmes ended the call and sighed. This was an unpleasant business from every angle, but he would see his little brother through it. After all, he was more than just a best man, he was first and foremost, Thomas's big brother. Only by a year, as Thomas kept reminding him, but still.

If Thomas had just listened to him in the first place, things wouldn't have gotten this far. Don't rush. Make sure that you're sure. There's time. He'd said all those things and more, but they'd fallen on deaf ears. The boy was blinded by what he thought was love.

Daniella came from a family with nothing. Traditionally, the bride's family would carry the cost of most of the wedding, but Thomas knew they couldn't and had been happy to draw on family money to foot the bill.

Benedict had no trouble with people who didn't have much. He and Thomas had had their fair share of that growing up. He even liked Daniella. The girl had a good heart. What tipped the scale toward the side of doubt was a single conversation he'd had with Thomas.

Only one, but it was enough.

People would judge him for the stance he'd taken, but Benedict faced the results of quick decisions and bad choices daily in his line of work and he'd seen the devastating consequences. He wanted more for his brother, and more for Daniella, too.

Thomas was heartbroken now, but he'd get over it. Benedict was about to make the next phone call when a message came through.

The Paper List: Re Thomas Holmes wedding card services. There is an outstanding matter to be discussed. Can we meet? Sincerely, Emma Redwood

Benedict felt tension ripple through his shoulders. He wanted to resolve everything to do with this disaster so that Thomas could put it all behind him and move on. It wouldn't do to have things like this coming back to cause problems. He'd meet the woman, but it would be on his terms.

Benedict: I'll be at the Coastline Yacht Club at 1 pm today.

He hit send.

• • • ● • ● • • •

Emma stretched, wobbled on the tips of her toes but still couldn't reach the birdseed on the top shelf. She glanced around, hunting for something to climb on, or a tall supermarket worker.

She tucked the small pile of narrow strips of paint samples into her bag to free up both hands as if that would somehow help her reach the birdseed. Emma had a deep love for paint samples that some would call an obsession. She couldn't walk past the colorful display in a paint section without taking a few. It wasn't just the colors (which made her happy) but it was the names of the colors that really did it for her.

The samples she'd taken from the paint section today were all in shades of blue. *Periwinkle Twinkle, Bluesy Woozy, Shimmering Sky.* She'd add them to her growing collection at home. That's of course if she ever found a way to reach the birdseed.

This was taking too long, she needed to get home and think about what to wear to face Benedict Holmes. She stretched up again as if she'd somehow grown taller in the last few seconds. It would have to be something power-*suity*, but less obvious. An outfit that clearly warned him not to mess with her.

A muscled arm reached in front of her nose and tapped the packet of birdseed.

"Just one?" The words were right in her ear, close enough to make her hair move. A voice so deep it made her belly flip.

"Aah, yes. Thank you." She turned towards her helper to grace him with a thank you smile. *Goodness, Lord, you certainly outdid Yourself with this one.* Dressed for a workout, the man was all broad, lean muscle.

He smiled at her as he placed the packet of birdseed in her hands. "They don't plan these shelves very cleverly, now do they?"

Warmth washed over her and she had to lock her knees not to sway. It had been a very long time since anyone had had this effect on her.

"Apparently short people don't care about birds."

"And tall people do. Didn't you know that?" He shrugged. "Anyway, anything else you need while I'm here? A new bin, perhaps?" He waved towards the other aisle where neat rows of colorful plastic bins lined the top shelf waiting to be taken home by tall people and filled with rubbish.

"My garbage needs are covered, but thanks anyway."

"Glad to hear it." He tipped an imaginary hat, "Enjoy the rest of your day." He left her in the aisle feeling a bit disorientated.

Emma shook her head to clear it and wiped the smile off her face. *Focus, girl.* She made her slow way to the checkout queue and stood there running mental lists.

"So what kind of bird do you have?" The voice slid down her spine like liquid velvet. He was back. Trust the man to pick her line.

Emma couldn't decide whether she wanted to run away, or stay in the line forever so she could keep listening to the low rumble of his voice.

The lady ahead of her was doubled-over by years, gnarled fingers painstakingly digging coins out of her purse and sliding them across to the cashier one at a time. This might well take forever.

"I don't have a bird, just a bird-*feeder*." Her eyes ran across the things in his basket. Full roast, extra strength Arabian coffee beans, a packet of peanuts, and some apples.

"A bird feeder, you say. That tells me a lot about you." He smiled knowingly and Emma resisted the urge to fold her arms across her chest.

"Excuse me? You don't know anything about me." She risked a quick glance at him and felt heat in her cheeks.

"True." He nodded once and even though he was agreeing with her, it felt like she was stuck behind an x-ray screen at an airport. The coin-counting lady had nearly paid half her bill. The cashier's eyes had glazed over and he stifled a yawn behind his hand.

Bird-seed tall man frowned at the slow-moving line, then shrugged it off and turned back to Emma. "Tell me if I'm wrong. You don't like having control over other people or things, but you are terrified of losing control over your own life."

"Isn't that everybody, though?" She schooled her mouth to a tight line.

"I guess so." His head tilted slightly to the side and he tapped his temple. "I think something is going on that you feel quite desperate about, and the only way for you to cling to normality is by immersing yourself in the mundane and caring for helpless things such as wild birds in your garden."

Emma was saved from responding by the coin-counting lady. She miraculously had counted out enough coins to redeem her few things. The coins didn't quite cover a packet of digestive biscuits which she slid off to one side a little sadly. Curling her fingers around the handles of her shopping bag, she shuffled off into the fast-moving morass of bodies.

Emma wondered about adding the biscuits to her bill and taking them to the lady, but before she could act on the thought, birdseed man slid a note toward the cashier and motioned for the packer to take them to the lady, who'd covered a surprising distance with her slow steps.

Emma felt both cheated and impressed. She threw down the seed with more force than necessary and paid.

"I'm not wrong, you know it." The tall man's voice was strangely gentle and it undid her tightly coiled emotions.

Emma took a deep breath, gathered up her seed, and met his eyes, "I guess we'll never know, now will we?" She shot him a sweet, thoroughly fake smile, and bolted.

• • • ● • ● • • •

Benedict watched until she walked outside and the sunlight caught in her blonde hair, an irresistible gleam of gold. Why did he always do that? Just because he knew things instinctively, didn't mean he had to say them out loud. He unpacked his items and reached for his card to pay.

The cashier followed his gaze. "You should have got her number, she's quite a catch."

Benedict frowned and thought of seven cutting things he could say to put this nobody back in his place but all that came out was, "She is, isn't she?"

Chapter Two

EMMA STEPPED INTO THE club and brushed off the feelings of inferiority that nibbled at her like hungry piranhas. Even breathing the air felt like it should cost per lungful. After being psycho-analyzed by a stranger in the checkout line, she'd lost her keys and spent the better part of an hour hunting for them.

That had thrown her timing out and she found herself outside the yacht club, ready to face the arrogant Mr. Holmes without anything remotely power-suity. The jeans she wore were probably her oldest and holiest, usually reserved for when she worked at home where nobody would see or emergency shop trips like the earlier birdseed run. Her sneakers? Well, they matched.

This was not how she planned for things to go down. There was nothing for it, but to go boldly. So what if she wore jeans and sneakers? There was more to her than her work clothes and Mr. Holmes was about to find that out.

She tucked her hair behind her ears and looked around.

The concierge appeared at her elbow. Everything about the man whispered discreetly. He was so proper, it made her want to crank up the music and dance on a table.

"Can I help you, Miss? If you're here about the waitress job, I can show you the right entrance?"

Emma regarded the man with cool eyes and felt her back straighten an extra fraction. "I'm meeting with Benedict Holmes."

The man tipped his head, then led her through the dark interior out onto a deck. Emma braced herself for meeting the insufferable Benedict Holmes. His brother, the bridegroom Thomas, was slim, bordering on skinny. Emma had never met him in person, but she'd seen a few photos on social media.

She'd been expecting an older version of skinny Thomas, but judging from behind, big brother Benedict was anything by slim. He had an innate athleticism about him that was obvious even covered by a fine linen shirt.

It made sense. That gravelly voice on the phone had to come from somewhere.

"Mr Holmes?" The man turned and Emma felt her insides twist. Birdseed man.

Emma sat in the chair the concierge pulled out for her.

Holmes glanced up as if he'd only just noticed her. "Aah, Miss Redwood? Can I get you a drink?"

"Tea, please."

"Tea for the lady and a regular for me. Thank you, Valentino."

He waited for the concierge to be out of earshot. "I trust the birds were happy with your purchase?"

"Oh you know birds, they never stop flitting long enough to leave a review." She took in the scenery to avoid meeting his eyes. He'd at least changed out of his gym clothes. "It's beautiful here."

The deck was built over the water. It gave the feeling of being on a boat, but without the seasick-inducing rocking. Being rich had its perks.

Benedict cleared his throat. "So, apart from taking care of wild birds, let me get this straight. You are one of the wedding suppliers that I had to cancel yesterday?"

Was this man dim? He'd spoken to her himself. "That's right. Wedding cards, name tags, that sort of thing."

"Right. What can I do for you?"

"I'm just going to be upfront and speak my mind if that's okay with you?"

His cool eyes regarded her with a slow flick. "It's the best way to do business, in my opinion."

Emma nodded, bundled her courage up into a tight ball, and blurted it out. "I want your help to get this wedding back on track."

He pulled back as if she'd waved a week-old dead fish under his nose. "Excuse me?"

"Thomas and Daniella. Their wedding shouldn't be canceled."

Benedict's mouth was a tight, straight line. "I'm sorry but that's not your call to make."

Emma drew a ragged breath. This man was formidable but she was determined. "Let me try and explain where I'm coming from. I deal with a lot of engaged couples. I can usually tell within the first five minutes which couples will work and which are going to fall apart."

"You see yourself as some sort of wedding prophet. Nice. As I understand it, you never even met them in person." His sarcasm smacked so hard, she thought it might leave a mark.

"I'm right ninety percent of the time." She shrugged. She wasn't bragging, it was pure facts. "Anyway, when Thomas contacted me about their wedding, I had the most overwhelming sense of rightness. They were one of the couples I pegged to make it. Which is why your call yesterday came as such a shock."

"Miss Redwood, rest assured that it came as a shock to all of us. Now, as soon as you show me the signed copy of your terms and conditions, I'll see to it that you are paid according to the agreement."

"Terms and conditions? I trust people. I don't make my clients sign anything."

Benedict's face did a weird little pull that made him look rather ugly. "Then there's nothing to discuss. I hope that you at least come out of this with some ideas to improve your good business practice."

Emma stared at him, studying him for a chink in the armor. Their drinks arrived and he poured tea for her while she scrambled for something to bait him with. In the back of her mind, she pictured the soggy bowls of ripped paper, waiting to be processed into the two love-birds wedding invitations.

"You are Thomas's best man, am I right?"

"Well I was, until yesterday."

"Part of your job as best man is to look after the groom. That includes helping him get over his cold feet. Did he say what the trouble was?"

The man might as well be a rock for the lack of budging. "Not that this is any of your business, I for one, happen to be relieved that they've come to their senses." He sniffed and stared down his nose at her. "They are both far too young to be thinking about a commitment like marriage. It seems to be the latest craze these days—try it and see if it works, if it doesn't, oh well, get a divorce and move on to the next one." His eyes met hers briefly. "Call me old-fashioned, but that commitment isn't one to be made lightly."

Emma slid back in her chair and crossed her arms. There was no ring on the man's finger. "Oh, I agree with you, but I think I can see what the problem is." Her eyes drifted pointedly to his empty ring finger. "He's your younger brother and he's settling down before you. I get it now. You can't handle the thought of it. Well, I think you should put your brother's welfare first for a change, and not your own."

If his face was a weather vane, she'd be diving for storm cover. She'd never seen a man this angry before.

"You are meddling in things you know nothing about." There was a dangerous quiet to his voice that should have warned her.

"And maybe you know too much and it's blinding you."

"Miss Redwoo—"

She put a hand on his arm. "Just think about it. Your little brother could be giving up on his shot at happiness, and you could be helping him."

Emma reached for her cup of tea, but couldn't bring herself to drink any. It wouldn't go down past the lump of broiling emotion in her throat. She slid a business card across the table, gathered up her things, and walked out.

• • • ● • ● • • •

Benedict watched her go with unease in his gut. Of course, it would be the woman from the shop with her holey jeans and her hair that tamed sunlight.

Here she was, meddling in things she had no business meddling in.

He'd had reservations about this wedding from the start. Thomas had only just graduated and hadn't yet found a job. Daniella was a sweet girl, but she was still studying. Social work was a noble choice but it wasn't going to pay enough for them to make a living. They really could do with some time. There was no reason to rush.

But Thomas was pushing for this wedding and Benedict had gone along with all of it. Until now. Their conversation and the unravelling of the relationship had seemed like an answer from Heaven.

But now this Emma woman was meddling and had her sights set on causing trouble.

Benedict drummed his fingers on the table. He'd have to watch her carefully. She had trouble written all over her. He mulled over what he knew about her, sifting through details and weighing it all up.

She'd gone shopping for a single pack of wild birdseed. Any other person would have gathered up a few other things while they were at it. From that one thing, he could tell that it was clear she needed the money.

Valentino came into the room discreetly to remove the untouched tea. "Is everything alright, sir?"

"Life is never simple, is it?"

Valentino's mask of professionalism gave way to the slightest chuckle. "Never. But problem-solving is satisfying. I'm sure you'll do the right thing, sir." He withdrew leaving Benedict to his thoughts.

Benedict's mind slid sideways and connected dots. He was about to start interviewing for a new project. She needed money and he needed someone to run his new project for him.

Maybe he could kill two birds with one stone.

Chapter Three

EMMA PICKED OUT A smooth rock and held it in her hand, wondering what she should paint. Her friends sat around a long table with open tubs of paint, paintbrushes, and rocks everywhere. A quiet hum of conversation filled the air.

Emma had joined the *Rock Our City* group on a dare. Her friend had told her of the strange concept of rock planting and Emma had shaken her head, called it weird, and brushed it off, but her friend then tossed out a patronizing comment that it was fine, Emma wouldn't get it anyway.

That level of snark had pushed Emma over the edge and she'd decided on the spot that, not only was she going to go to a rock painting session, she was going to have an absolute ball doing it.

To her surprise, she'd been going back ever since even though her friend had left town and didn't go anymore. It was an odd mix of people but it was cathartic to paint rocks, hide them all over the city, then watch random strangers post on social media when they found them.

Friendships in the group were easy. Nobody ever asked to meet outside their weekday painting date, or their occasional trip around the city to plant rocks.

Emma turned the rock over in her palm waiting for inspiration to strike.

Vicky slid into the chair next to her with her current rock in hand. "Win this argument for me,"—she held out a rock in her hand. "I think this one should be a hedgehog, but Kerry over there says a small fox."

Emma shrugged. "Which one would you prefer to paint? I think that's the better question."

Vicky bounced the rock in her palm. "Good point. Hedgehog it is, sorry Kerry."

Emma applied the same logic to her rock and settled on a moonrise over water. She picked out brushes that would fit the thickness of the lines she needed and annexed the blue, white, and black tubs of paint. It took away from all the thoughts churning in her head about rent, broken engagements, and an infuriating best man who didn't know how to do his job properly.

Without thinking too much, she sketched in pencil lines on the smooth surface and started to paint.

"So Emma, I saw you getting cozy with Benedict Holmes at the yacht club. What's going on? Come on, do tell." It was busy-body Brenda. Of course. Brenda ran their rock club but she was also a well-established art curator with a gallery that had helped launch many local artists into the spotlight.

None of that made her fun to be around though.

Emma's paintbrush splattered paint across her rock, ruining her careful artwork. Of course it would be Brenda asking, the one woman in the group that Emma had never really connected with. Looking at her now, with her plastered-on smile and dyed black hair, Emma felt a strong dislike of the woman take root inside of her.

A couple of the other ladies' head's bobbed up from their paintbrushes.

Emma shrugged. "Just a client. One who is trying to do me out of my money, I might add." She allowed a little venom to trickle into her tone to neutralize any romantic ideas brewing in the room.

Brenda nodded knowingly, with a smug little grin that made the papery skin on her cheeks all wrinkly. "Alright, if you say so."

Awkward silence settled over the room and Brenda kept shooting little knowing glances at Emma with her mouth twisted in a knowing smirk. Five minutes of it was all Emma could take.

She checked her watch. "Well, will you look at the time? I'd better run." She rinsed off her brushes and packed up faster than you could say *hush up Brenda*.

• • • • ● • ● • • • •

Benedict had just paid for coffee at his favorite street-side vendor when he saw Miss Emma Redwood exiting the building across the road rather speedily. Her face was flushed, her steps were short and clipped—angry walking, he would guess.

He sipped the hot, black, liquid and watched her cross the road. She stepped off the curb straight in front of an oncoming car and didn't skip a beat when the driver honked the horn. She threw up a flat palmed hand as if to *say get out of my face*.

Her anger only deflated when she got to her car and found a flat tire. He kept watching while she pounded the roof with her fists, then switched to rubbing her temples as if her head was about to split open from pain.

He drained the last sip of his coffee, threw away the cup, and sauntered over to her. "Do you need some help?"

Emma glanced at him and threw her hands in the air. "Perfect. Just perfect." Her eyes narrowed dangerously. "Did you do this?" Then her face changed as if he'd said yes when in reality he'd done nothing but offer help. "You did this."

"Miss Redwood, I have better things to do with my time. I am happy to help you change it, if you would like me to."

She opened her mouth to say no, he watched her lips form the word, but before she could say anything, he cut in.

"It would be a shame to get dirt on that pretty white top of yours."

Emma's head tilted to the side. "And what about your fancy shirt? Hmm?"

He plucked at it. "This old thing? It's a step away from a rag anyway. Come on, let's get you going again."

She popped the trunk and he dug around inside for the spare and tools. One look at the spare and he knew they had a problem. "This spare is the wrong one for this car. It won't fit."

"That's impossible. It came with the car."

"Did you buy this as a used car?" Benedict eyed the car critically.

"Not used, *pre-loved*. There's a big difference. I don't see how that would affect the spare." She stopped and suddenly seemed full of doubt. "Surely?"

"Well, this one isn't going anywhere. I'll take you to get a new one." He watched the expressions play across her features and shook his head as she started to make an excuse. "Come on. It's not a big deal."

He bundled her into the car and they drove off under the watchful eyes of a group of ladies peering out an upstairs window.

• • • • ● • ● • • •

A sick realization hit Emma as they pulled up to the tire shop. There was no way she had enough money in the bank to pay for a new tire.

Stuck. Stuck. Stuck. Now what?

Benedict pulled up and stopped the car and Emma grabbed her only chance to avoid the deep embarrassment that waited for her inside.

"Thanks for the lift. I'll just take it from here." Her mind flew through her friend list. Who could she phone who'd be able to come over to bail her out, and help her fit a new tire?

Benedict regarded her with absolute calm and climbed out of the car.

Emma was mortified. She had to think fast. "Oh no! I didn't bring my wallet. We can't do this now. Maybe you can drop me off back at the car and I'll make another plan."

To her horror, he ignored her suggestion and waved her into the shop before him. "Don't stress. We can sort it out later."

Emma dragged her feet, wishing the earth would eat her up. This was not a good way to prove that she was level-headed and quite able to take care of herself. She was a strong, independent woman, for goodness sake!

By the time she'd forced herself to go inside, Benedict was sitting paging through a car magazine. "I've ordered and paid for a new tire. They're fetching it from the stores out back. We have to wait for a few minutes."

All the chairs in the waiting area were full and Emma was forced to sit next to squeeze in next to the man on a tiny two-seater.

"You must let me have your bank details." She was proud of the fact that her voice held steady, even though her insides shook. "What kind did you order?"

"The non-flat kind." There was no mistaking the quick pull to his lip even though he quickly got it under control.

"A joke. I'm impressed. You almost smiled." The feeling of being beholden to him made her squirm. Emma needed to earn more and fast. She didn't want to owe this man anything. "I have a question for you. Why are you helping me?"

Emma asked the question then forced herself to silence. Usually, in situations like this, she'd just keep blurting out things to try and make it feel more comfortable. She bit her lips to hold in all the words.

"Does there have to be a reason?"

"Yes, out with it."

Silence stretched to the point that she wondered if he'd forgotten that she was waiting.

"Fine. The truth is, I need a favor."

Chapter Four

THE MOON WAS ALREADY high in the sky when Emma unlocked her front door. She was weary from the top of her aching head to the soles of her tired feet.

Benedict had stubbornly refused to elaborate on the favor he required, but had instead, driven her around the city looking at run-down old houses. She'd stopped counting after the third one. They didn't go inside but merely pulled up, had a quick look while he sprouted random facts, then went on to the next one.

He wouldn't answer any of her questions and eventually, she gave up asking. Not knowing what he wanted had set her on high alert and she'd struggled to pay attention to each house.

Despite that, one, in particular, had caught her interest with its high, vaulted ceilings, enormous glass windows, and, apparently, a mini terrarium right in the middle of the house. A living garden right in the middle of a house. The concept delighted her.

Afterward, he'd dropped her at home and cryptically told her to keep thinking of the houses, and he'd be in touch soon.

She was tempted to yell out *why* as he was leaving, but he wouldn't have answered anyway. So she settled for sticking out her tongue at his retreating back. It was altogether unsatisfying.

She settled in the living room with a cup of tea and checked her email, hoping for some new wedding card business. Instead, there was an email from Benedict.

Miss Redwood,
Follow the link to an online quiz. Please complete it before 9 a.m. tomorrow.
Regards,
Benedict Holmes

What? The nerve of the man! Why would she even consider it?

She powered down her laptop and brushed her teeth before bed. But through it all, her mind turned the email over and over. She'd already climbed under the covers when curiosity got the best of her and she logged in on her phone.

The link took her to a simple, online quiz.

The first question showed photos of three different living rooms and the question was simply *pick one*. The first picture was a glamorous living room in shades of red, black, and gold. It was opulent and rich, but way too over the top for her taste.

The second picture showed a classy living room, all French deco in muted shades of white. It was easy on the eyes, looked expensive, but felt cold, and showed no character.

The third photo took Emma's breath away. It was simple and clean, with a warm white base, but splashes of jewel colors gave it warmth and homeliness that made her happy.

She clicked to choose the third one and frowned a little, expecting the worst for the next one. But what followed was an endless selection of chairs, furniture, paint colors, finishes, and everything else to do with home interiors.

It was weird but relaxing, and Emma finished it off in no time at all. There you go, Benedict. It was after midnight when she shot off an answer to his email. No frills or small-talk, just a quick *all done*.

Curiosity would surely be the end of her.

She drifted off to sleep amidst floating chairs, chaises, and fine linen.

• • • ● • ● • • •

Benedict forced himself to eat breakfast. He had a wild plan and it wasn't in his nature to second guess himself once he'd decided on a course of action. But this? This was a risk that involved including other people and that always made him think twice.

He'd been praying more of late, and it seemed to soothe the sting of indecision. He was not a religious man, but he did speak to God regularly and he believed that God had looked out for him at the most significant times of his life. Who knew what God truly thought anyway?

Praying now seemed like the right thing to do, so he lifted his thoughts heavenwards, waiting for any sign that he was on the right track.

His laptop woke up on cue and proceeded to download email. He heard the blip of at least a dozen emails come through and opened up to check. First on the list was a reply from Emma. She'd responded after midnight. Either the girl was a raving insomniac, or she was the right kind of dedicated worker he wanted on his team.

He clicked through to see her answers to the quiz he'd set. The next step was to determine whether or not her natural taste would be suitable for the project he had in mind. If it did, and if she accepted his proposal, he'd have the perfect excuse to keep her right under his watchful eye. He'd keep her so busy, she would forget all about Thomas, all about the botched wedding, and her own, incorrect, wedding prophecies.

He found himself nodding as he clicked through her choices. Her taste was modern, with a luxury edge to a comfortable, homely feel. Perfect.

It was time for the last test. He messaged her a single question—which house do you choose?

He watched the line across his phone display as she typed her response.

Emma: I liked the third one best.

No hesitation, no explanation. Just how he liked it.

Of course, she would pick the third one with all its awkward secrets. Maybe it was God's way of saying it was time.

Right Emma Redwood, you've passed the test. Now to get you to agree with me. There was nothing that fired him up as much as a challenge did, and this woman was proving to be suitably challenging.

He dialed her number.

• • • ● • ● • • •

Emma answered the call without checking who was calling and instantly regretted it when she heard Benedict's voice.

"Miss Redwood, I have a proposal for you. Be ready in thirty minutes."

Emma coughed at the audacity of the man. "I'm sorry, I'm not available today." *Or ever.* But what if she could get into this man's head? Figure him out and change his mind about the wedding?

Emma grabbed the closest book and held the phone near enough to pick up the sound of her paging through it, then she shoved the phone back to her ear. It was a lame trick, more suited to old romance movies and high school crushes.

She cringed at her actions. *Grow up, Emma.*

"Will you look at that? I've just had a cancellation. I'll be ready."

"Great." He ended the call and Emma flopped on her favorite chair.

She caught sight of her fluffy P.J. pants and panicked. She checked the time, only twenty-five minutes until the man would be here to fetch her.

In defiance of his tidy suits, she reached for her standard jeans, t-shirt, and sneakers. She splashed water on her face, ignored her make-up, and scraped her hair back into a tight ponytail.

After a few seconds of feeling the pull, she thought better of that hairstyle and switched to a loose plait. She tested it with a quick headshake. No impending headache ... much better.

By the time she was done, she still had seven minutes to kill until the man arrived to fetch her. She peeped out the window and saw his car parked below. For a split second, she thought about making him wait for her but, once again, curiosity got the better of her and she headed downstairs to meet him.

• • • • ● • ● • • •

Now that he had Emma in the car with him, Benedict couldn't quite figure out how he was going to make his offer. They drove to the third house in thick silence.

Emma sat quietly, with her arms folded, staring out the window at the houses as they flew past.

She shot a quick look at him and their eyes met before they both looked away.

"I'm guessing you're not going to tell me what I'm doing here or what this mysterious proposal is."

Benedict could feel her eyes on him. "All in good time. I do need to ask you one thing though. Is the wedding card business your only source of income?"

"That's a rather personal question, don't you think?" Color flooded her cheeks.

"Indulge me. I'm not asking from idle curiosity."

"Fine. For the moment, yes. I have other ideas, but I have to build up capital first." She sniffed. "How about you?"

Benedict swallowed a laugh. This girl was full of spunk. "Well, that's turning the tables. I have multiple streams of income, yes. I don't believe in the whole philosophy of many eggs and one basket. I don't think that's a safe way to live." He took a deep breath. "So if I offered you another source of income, would you consider it?"

She shifted in her seat, the question made her uneasy. "It depends. I'm not going to do anything I wouldn't be willing to tell my grandma about, if you get my meaning."

Benedict couldn't keep the laugh in this time, it exploded out of him. "That's so quaint. The thing is, you'll be sworn to secrecy and for very good reason."

• • • ● • ● • • •

Emma felt the silence as a tangible thing hovering between them, mocking her rash decision to come on this trip. They'd left the city behind and were traveling on quieter roads that snaked through the country.

Just before her panic erupted out of her mouth as a shrill scream, Benedict pulled up outside what she recognized to be, the third house. The house she'd chosen from the others.

"Why are we here?"

Benedict smiled and the change in his face was quite a thing to behold. "Come, we'll chat inside." He led the way to the front door and unlocked it.

Emma walked slowly, studying the patchy lawn, the broken railing that surrounded the porch. "This place is quite rundown. Is it yours?"

Benedict shook his head and held a finger to his lips. "Let's take a quiet walk through the house. I don't want you to talk. Just take it in. Yes?"

"Fine. You seem to enjoy drama."

He leaned in close, tapped his finger on his mouth, and said, "Shh!"

Emma frowned but followed him into the house. The place was in bad shape. Not just dirty, but neglected too. "This a wreck."

He spun around and frowned at her and she threw up her hands and whispered, "Sorry."

The house centered around an internal terrarium, but the glass windows were too dirty to see much of what was going on inside. The door they walked past looked as if hadn't been opened in years and Benedict showed no signs of trying.

As they walked, Emma found her mind working on two separate tracks. On the one side, she was already making mental notes of what she'd repair or replace if the house were hers.

On the other, her imagination woke up and she saw the house restored, gleaming under the loving care of someone with a bit of flair and a good, solid, lump of cash. Each room came alive in her mind, all except the last one.

Their walk took them around the outside of the house through an overgrown jungle of a garden where she noticed a rough door that led to the cellar. It was padlocked shut with a rusty lock. For some reason, that room bothered her, and the urge to see inside swept over her like an overwhelming flood.

She tapped Benedict on the shoulder and pointed at her mouth with a questioning shrug.

"You want to talk?"

"Yes! Why is this door locked? What happened here? It feels like some sort of crime scene. Can we go inside?"

Benedict shrugged. "That's not why we're here. What do you think of the rest of this place?"

Emma glanced at the door that defied her. "This room bothers me. Apart from this one, I think the house is gorgeous. It needs a ton of work and money, but it would be beautiful."

"Good. That's what I was hoping you'd say. I'd like to employ you to restore it."

• • • ● • ● • • •

Emma sat in the lounge of her rental house with her mind reeling. What Benedict proposed seemed like an offer she couldn't possibly refuse. But it didn't stop her wondering what the man was up to and why. Should she or shouldn't she? That was the big question.

Just then a text from her bank came through notifying her that the account was overdrawn. There were no more wedding card orders on email either. Up until now, Jesus had been kind enough to provide a steady stream of work.

Well, 'stream' was probably too generous a word. More like a trickle. But she'd always seemed to have had at least one more job lined up before finishing whatever she'd been working on.

The truth was, many brides were opting for an electronic invitation and RSVP service. Few wanted to go to the expense of luxury paper and envelopes, with calligraphy in fine gold ink.

Clearly, she was a dinosaur in a world of handbag dogs.

The mental image of a T-Rex shredding paper and gold flakes popped up in her head and she groaned.

Someone knocked on the door and Emma's first thought was Benedict, but she opened to find her landlord with an elderly couple queuing up behind him, clearly expecting her to let them in.

"Miss Redwood, I'm assuming you got my email?"

Her landlord was a young woman, so young, she looked as if she should rather still be in school. She was clearly aware of it and dressed in a tweed suit in an ugly shade of olive and low-heeled, closed shoes to compensate. Her hair was scraped back into a low bun in the nape of her neck which made her look like a kid all ready for dress-as-your-parent day.

She was on a mission to prove her competence and Emma seemed to be her target of choice.

"Your rent is now overdue for the second time. I'm sure I don't need to remind you of our strict defaulter policy." She waved towards the couple behind her. "I'll be showing the Bernsteins around."

It wasn't a request so much as information for Emma to absorb and make peace with.

If things carried on like this, she'd lose her home.

Her phone beeped again.

Benedict: I forgot to mention, I'd need you to move into the house while the renovation is happening. If you're interested, I'll send over a contract for signature.

Emma felt cornered, ganged up on. She typed as fast as her fingers could go.

Emma: I have questions before I can make my final decision. Should I email them?

His reply was quick.

Benedict: I'll pick you up at 8 for a working dinner. That will give us plenty of time to discuss everything that you need to know.
P.S. Dress smart.

Emma threw down the phone in disgust. She didn't want to dress smart, she didn't want to discuss anything with the man face-to-face and most of all, she didn't want to have to sit through an entire meal with the man.

But it would seem, she was out of options.

Mrs Bernstein chose that moment to stick her head into the room. "Thank you, dear, for letting us have a look around. Your roses are lovely! I think we'll definitely be taking the place." She graced Emma with a smile as if she were doing Emma the biggest favor.

Emma waited until she heard the gate clang behind them before letting out a frustrated growl.

She stormed to the cupboard, yanked out her standard little black dress, sparkly heels and drop earrings. Her hair would go up in an elegant French roll, held in place with diamante pins. If Benedict wanted smart, he would get smart.

She'd even dust off her deep red lipstick.

Chapter Five

THOMAS WAS EATING CEREAL for supper and doodling in a sketchbook at the kitchen counter when Benedict came down the stairs ready to go fetch Emma.

"You're looking smart. Big date?" Thomas was a mess. His hair hadn't been brushed in days, his scraggly beard was taking advantage of the absence of a razor and seemed to be growing as quickly as possible as if trying to prove that it could.

"Have you been sleeping? You look terrible." Benedict buttoned his cuffs and pulled his jacket straight.

"Eh, who needs sleep." Thomas shrugged his skinny shoulders. "I should come with you. It would get me out the house." He grinned as he said it, but Benedict got the feeling he was actually dead serious.

"It's okay bud. Maybe spend tonight catching up on personal hygiene and grooming." Benedict winked at him. "It won't be a long night out anyways. Should we find a movie to watch later?"

Thomas looked less than convinced. "I don't know if I'm up to staying here alone by myself. Not even for a short dinner."

"You'll be fine, it's not that long. I'll take my phone in case you need me. How does that sound?"

"Sure, go off and leave me. I'm just the little brother after all." He picked up his pencil and turned to one of the few blank pages left in a tattered sketchbook.

Benedict glanced at it with a frown. That book seemed to go wherever Thomas did. "You know, if you spent half as much time paying attention to real life as you did doodling in that thing, you'd be making a decent living by now."

"Doing what? I don't want to do anything else." Thomas didn't even look up, fixated on the tip of his pencil moving across the off-white paper.

"Are you serious? You can't live on trust fund money for the rest of your life. That's not how it works."

"You don't have a job either. I don't see *you* earning money."

"Just because I don't discuss my work with you, doesn't mean it doesn't exist. Besides, I'm smart. There are ways of earning money outside of a mere salary." Benedict checked his watch, the conversation was taking too long.

"So you're implying I'm not smart. Thanks."

Benedict ruffled his hair and pulled as his fingers got caught in a tangle. "Bro, that's disgusting. Wash your hair, please. I'll be back later."

"You're not my mother," Thomas yelled out as Benedict left the house.

Benedict drove to Emma's apartment with a knot in his stomach. Thomas wasn't doing well and there was only so much he could do about it. Thomas was swiftly booted out of his mind when Emma appeared at the door.

He'd only ever seen her in jeans. Emma in an evening dress looked so different, that he had to double-take to make sure it was her.

He held the car door open for her. "You clean up nicely."

She glanced at him briefly before answering, "So do you."

The restaurant he'd booked at was close by, which was a good thing because Emma was so fidgety, she might as well be sitting on an ant nest by the time they arrived.

"Your usual seat, sir?"

Benedict barely had to tip his head for the waiter to usher them through to the most private spot in the place. The colors were warm shades of muted maroon and gold. Discreet music, low lighting, just how he liked it.

"So, you have questions?" The waiter left with their drinks order and Benedict turned to Emma.

Emma nearly bit her lip but must have changed her mind for the sake of not getting lipstick on her teeth. "I do."

"Shoot."

Emma sat straight in her chair, her bare back didn't touch the backrest of the chair. She tapped on the table between them with one finger. "Budget. Living expenses. Timeframe." She'd tapped a separate finger for each point. "I think that's a good start."

"Fair questions. I will meet with you once a week to discuss the budget for each section as we go. You will be paid a salary that will more than cover your living expenses. Timeframe? Six months to a year, though it's flexible."

"Sounds reasonable. Next question—why me?" Emma leaned back in her chair and looked him dead in the eye.

"Do you want the honest answer or the polite answer?" Benedict fought to keep a straight face.

Emma blinked at him. "Honest, obviously."

"This is a side project for me. My company keeps me busy, but this project is closer to my heart. Why you? Well, I wasn't fooled by the jeans and tees. I could tell by the wedding card sample that you sent that you have refined taste. The quiz I sent over confirmed that you naturally lean towards the style I have in mind. The clincher was how passionately you hunted me down to plead Thomas and Daniella's case. Misguided, in their case, but I think that would work on suppliers." He added as an afterthought, "Even though it didn't work on me."

Emma wasn't smiling. It was hard to read her expression.

"Also," he shifted in his seat, "I would like to replace the income you lost, but the businessman in me demands that it's a fair trade." *It also keeps you too busy to interfere with the two broken-hearted love birds.*

He kept the last explanation to himself. It wouldn't do for him to play his whole hand at once.

• • • ● ●• ● ● • • •

All through supper, Emma ran options in the back of her mind. Whichever way she looked at it, she came back to the fact that she had no other choice than to take on the challenge. Yet having no choice made her feel like a cornered animal.

She would have to give up her home, trust this man and his stone heart, and move on to his rundown property.

The vegetable lasagna she'd ordered was so good, yet she could barely manage more than a few mouthfuls. Her appetite had vanished.

She pushed her plate away. "Let me put it this way. The only dealings I've had with you were enough to single-handedly fold my business. Now I need to give up my home for a temporary place to stay, for a temporary job? I'm sorry if I don't seem excited."

"Emma, look at it this way, if one client letting you down is enough to close your business, you might need to have a serious look at whether there's enough market potential to keep going. You might love what you do, but it's probably going to have to give way to something more substantial. Maybe you can keep doing it as a hobby on the side."

His voice was deep and soothing but that only made it sting worse. Emma shut her eyes and rubbed circles on her temples, hoping it would chase her headache away.

"Can I trust you?"

Benedict stared into her eyes with a small frown resting in the crease between his eyebrows. "Are you seriously considering taking this on? No buts, just yes, or no?"

Even as Emma started thinking in circles again, she knew there was no other option. She nodded once.

Benedict gave a slight smile, pulled out his phone, and tapped a few taps on the screen. Emma's phone blipped and she pulled it out of her pocket to check.

A message arrived confirming a deposit of $2000 into her bank account and seconds later an email from the landlord came through confirming that the new tenants had signed a lease agreement and she needed to leave by month-end.

She shoved her phone at Benedict. "Is this money from you? Explain please."

"That should cover relocation and settling-in expenses. We'll order boxes on our way to drop you home. There'll be a moving truck over tomorrow lunchtime to pack up your things and take them across."

This was all moving so fast, Emma felt breathless. The irony of the situation was a bit much—right now she had enough money to pay her rent and stay on in the little house she loved so much, but she'd lost the opportunity by minutes.

She didn't want to be bullied, but if riding this wave bought her some time to get back on her feet, so be it.

"I'm ready. Bring it on."

Chapter Six

THE HOUSE WAS IN total chaos. Emma's apartment was tiny and she hadn't brought much, so she managed to fit her things into the one mostly intact room. That would be her living space until some of the other rooms were done.

The day had been long and tiring as she'd started before sunrise by emailing her landlord—ex-landlord—and spent the rest of the morning packing boxes. The truck arrived at midday and she'd watched a dozen men pack up the contents of her life in under an hour. Most of it went into storage and just the essentials were dropped off at the renovation house.

She'd packed up Thomas and Daniella's wedding card-makings herself and carefully placed that box on the passenger seat of her car. For some reason, she couldn't let go of the idea that those two were meant to be together.

Driving behind the truck to her new home felt surreal. The sun shone through the trees as if it were a most glorious day, but Emma's heart weighed heavy.

Another fifteen minutes and all her things stood stacked up against a wall of the one intact room.

She'd either been rescued or set up for disaster. There was no telling which.

The kitchen was semi-functioning, so she made a sandwich and tea, and settled on her bed to take stock.

There was more money in her bank than she'd seen in a while, she had a roof over her head, and a big project to tackle. That should be enough to set her heart at ease. But she missed her old rental with its vines and rose bushes. She took a moment to mourn the loss before forcing it all aside. Where she was now was nothing short of a miracle.

Focus on the miracle of it all.

And yet underneath it all lurked a fact that she didn't care to think about. All of this tied her to Benedict Holmes with strings that seemed unbreakable.

That thought alone scared her.

• • • ● • ● • • •

Benedict collected the pizza he'd ordered and drove to the house. Emma's car was parked in the drive and the lights were on inside the living room. Good. So far she was going along with the plan. There wasn't a working doorbell, so he settled for an old-fashioned knock on the front door.

Emma opened with the chain hooked and shut it again quickly before opening it up wide. "You coming to check on me already?"

He wiggled the box of hot pizza at her. "Just bringing supper. I don't know if you'd be able to cook in the kitchen yet." He led the way through the mess to the kitchen and threw the light switch.

The island in the middle of the square room was open, so he put the pizza down and turned a slow circle to examine the space.

Emma stood next to him, just reaching his shoulder. "This room has potential. I like it."

I like you in it. He swatted away the unwelcome thought. "I'm keen to see it when you're done."

Emma fetched two plates from a brown box labeled 'kitchen' and put one down on opposite sides of the island. "I'm assuming you're staying for supper? This is way too much for me to eat by myself."

Benedict hadn't been intending to stay, but her invitation and the smell of the food were enough to persuade him.

"Sure."

They sat down opposite each other and pulled out warm slices of the hot pizza.

He watched her eat with delicate fingers. "Can we talk business while we eat, or do you want to keep it for during the week?"

Emma shook her head. "I'm hoping to save as much time as I can for working during the day, so chat away."

"Have you thought about what order you'd like to tackle the rooms in?" Benedict took a bite and chewed while waiting for her to answer.

Emma reached for a notepad on the counter behind her and pulled a pencil out from behind her ear. "Functionally, I think either a bathroom or the kitchen. Those two are crucial for a functioning house. After that, I would go with the downstairs living room, then one of the bedrooms. What do you think?"

"Sounds good to me. So? Kitchen or bathroom. Which one first?"

Emma tapped her lip, thinking. "I feel like a bathroom would go quicker? So let me choose that first, then the kitchen."

Benedict reached into the bag he'd brought in, slipped his laptop onto the table, and fired it up. He reached in for a second time and came up with a second laptop which he placed in front of Emma. "There you go. This is yours. It has the project management software I use preloaded. I'm sure you can do with having something working well."

"Mine works, it's just a bit slow." She slid the new one a little closer back to him, reluctantly. It looked so sleek and new. Her *enter* key only worked on every third press, the space bar got stuck often and left big gaps of nothing in whatever she happened to be typing. Working on her old dinosaur was slowly driving her over the edge, but she just couldn't bring herself to accept anything more from Benedict.

"And now you don't have to have a slow one. Just use it, enjoy it." He slid it straight back to her. "No strings attached." He looked at her face and sighed. "Listen to me, this is about me, not you. I want to know that the tools you're using a completely reliable and aren't going to stop working halfway through. It's a company expense. Tax-deductible. You'll be doing me a huge favor by taking it."

"Fine. Thank you."

"I've loaded a budget on the spreadsheet program. You'll see the rough amounts I've allocated for each space. Please keep an open dialogue with me as you go."

Emma ran her hand through her hair. "No rules? Guidelines?"

Benedict seemed to brood over his words for a moment before responding. "Only one. Forget about the noble hopes you have for my brother and his ex-fiancée."

• • • • ● • ● • • •

Emma stirred the powder blue paint a little more violently than it needed to be. It would seem this whole elaborate setup was a ploy to get her off the track of reuniting Thomas and Daniella.

The man had overplayed his hand when he'd laid down the law. Emma never responded well to having her rights read to her and the urge to slap her hairy toe over the line he'd drawn in the sand was overwhelming.

She filled up a paint tray that she'd found amongst a stash of brand new supplies in the garage. Twenty minutes later, the *en-suite* had its first coat of paint and it was time for a tea break.

While she was waiting for the kettle to boil, she opened up her social media pages and typed in Thomas's name. She found his page easily, she knew it was him because it listed a 'Benedict' as a brother, and started scrolling. Most of his posts were all about Daniella. If the photos were anything to go by, it was deeply obvious that these two were smitten with each other.

Half of the photos had them staring at each other, the other half showed one of them focused elsewhere, but the other—without fail—staring at their unsuspecting other, adoringly. It went both ways.

How could Benedict not see this?

Wait.

She could go snoop around and see what she could find out about the man. Her mouse pointer hovered over his name, but she just couldn't bring herself to click. It seemed wrong, invasive.

With a sigh, she shut down her laptop and got back to work in the house. The paint was still tacky, so she took her clipboard and wandered from room to room, getting ideas and making notes.

Through it all, thoughts kept buzzing, mixed up with prayers sent heavenwards, and eventually, she settled on a conclusion.

She was going to investigate and find out as much as she could about those two. One of two things would happen: this deep sense of wrongness at their breakup would leave, or she would make moves to get them back together.

Despite what pompous Mr. Benedict Holmes might say.

Chapter Seven

BENEDICT TOWERED OVER THOMAS who lay curled up in bed. Benedict was dressed in running shorts and his legs felt the cold. The moment he got moving, he'd warm up, but for now, he was feeling the early morning chill and it was making him grumpy.

"What time is it?" Thomas squinted and blinked against the light Benedict had switched on.

"It's time to get moving, slug."

Thomas groaned and buried himself deeper under his duvet.

Benedict wasn't having any of it. "I'm not leaving until you get up."

Thomas threw back just enough of the duvet to glare at him. "I don't even run."

"Today's a good day to start." He injected a flinty steel tone he used on staff members who were caught hiving off. "Come on sunshine, let's go."

"I hate you. Do you know how much I hate you right now?"

Benedict tipped his head as if Thomas had complimented him.

By the time they hit the road the sun was lighting the horizon in a purple-orange haze.

Benedict ran a circle around disgruntled Thomas. "Keep up." He took off at his usual pace, reveling in the feeling of blood pumping through his system.

For a while, he was aware of Thomas's feet slapping the road behind him. It felt good to get his brother out of the house, he'd done the right thing bullying him. His mind wandered onto other things, such as his newest employee.

He thought she'd put up more of a fight about moving into the house, but maybe she was desperate. He felt a spike of warmth he usually felt when he did something right. Man, he was on a roll.

Benedict shot a glance backward to check on Thomas. The road behind stretched out empty, not a sign of his brother.

Thomas, you nit. Muttering under his breath, he spun around and back-tracked his steps. No sign of the boy. He got to a four-way stop and checked the road in both directions.

Something moved in the distance off to the left. He sped up and sprinted until he caught up. Thomas wasn't running. He trudged along with his shoulders slumped and his hands in his pockets.

"Hey, I told you to keep up. What's going on?"

Thomas shot him a dark glance and kept walking.

"Stop acting like a sulky teenager and talk to me."

Thomas spun towards him. His hands shot out his pockets into balled fists, then dropped to his sides. "And what good would that do? You never listen to me anyway."

Benedict dismissed his dramatic declaration. "Where are you going?" He looked up and saw that they were standing outside Daniella's apartment. "No. Thomas, pull yourself together."

Thomas stared at him, raised an eyebrow, and cracked out the fakest smile Benedict had ever seen. "Make me."

Benedict blinked, all his words gone. He raised both his hands and backed off. "All I'm trying to say is I don't even think she's home right now." The empty space in the parking lot below the apartment building was where Daniella's car would usually be. It was pure providence that he'd spotted it at that moment.

Thomas breathed in deeply, let it out slowly, and turned.

Benedict felt a rip of emotion through his insides. He hated being the rock and the hard place, but his brother needed him now.

He needed Benedict to be strong for him and make the hideously hard choices.

Lord, I don't know how You expect me to do this.

A wisp of bitterness slipped through the ache inside him. "Come on, let's go home."

• • • • ● • ● • • •

Emma spread her paint samples on the bed. She couldn't resist collecting them and now had so many, she'd had to buy a special box to store them all in. They'd always seemed significant, but a new thought had emerged since living in this house. What if ...

What if she picked out colors, matched them to people, and used them as prayer cards? The idea made her smile.

Dani felt like gentle shades of yellow. Emma found the perfect card and wrote a large D in her finest calligraphy in the middle of the top block. The shades of yellow were *friendly banana, smiles in sunlight, terrific taxicab, beach house door,* and *penguin belly.*

Thomas felt like blue, so she picked out a sample and wrote a T in the middle of a shade called *favorite mug*. The other blue tints on the card were *cloud watcher, crashing waves, the sparkle in your eye,* and *not green.*

A maroon one caught her eye for Benedict. She read the names and laughed. *Surfing bruise, wine stain on my least favorite shirt, handpicked berries, behind the velvet curtain,* and *delicious secrets*. Wow. Somehow, they all seemed appropriate.

Emma fluffed her pillow to lean on, placed the two colored cards next to her new laptop. She jiggled the trackpad and the laptop woke up. It was so much faster than her old one. Hers would take so long to start up that she'd usually go make a cup of tea while waiting.

She stretched and rolled her head, easing the stiffness out of her neck. She stopped dead, mid-roll, and stared at the ceiling. Right above her on the ceiling sat a spider. She jumped off the bed with a tiny shriek.

Of course, the bug spray was finished.

She grabbed her slipper and stood ready as if she were facing down a gunman ready to duel in an old-fashioned dusty Western movie. The spider sat calmly without moving a muscle. Maybe it wasn't hunting her down.

It didn't help that the ceilings in this place were high enough that any attempt at removing the trespasser would likely result in it falling on her face. Emma stretched out and snatched the paint samples and laptop off her bed.

She wasn't going to let an eight-legged critter throw her off.

The room had a large bay window that overlooked the mess of a garden, so she settled on the generous sill and felt warmth from the sun seep into her.

Right, Lord. Where should I start?

She opened up *Instagram*. A quick search later, she'd found Daniella's page. The girl hadn't posted much recently.

Her highlights had a section called 'Date Nights.'

Emma felt weird going through the photos, but anything posted on a public platform was fair game. So she scrolled pages of Thomas and Dani, looking happy and relaxed, taking walks, climbing trees, chasing sunsets, and rescuing bees from drowning. Apparently, they both had a soft spot for bees.

Everything she saw left her more convinced than before that Dani and Thomas should never have split up. She took her Dani and Thomas cards, held them in her hands, and started praying.

• • • • • • • • • •

Benedict scanned the shelves for a replacement door handle. The one on the bathroom door had been getting worse and had stopped working altogether this morning. Thomas had got himself trapped inside and it had taken much muscle power to get him out.

The bruise on Benedict's shoulder was going to be a doozy.

He picked out what he wanted and turned in time to see Emma breezing past the aisle he was in.

She looked completely out of place in a hardware store in her flowing skirt that caught the wind as she walked.

It was a good thing he saw her. If she were here to buy things for the house, he could help. An old couple blocked the aisle with their shopping cart as they argued over a light fitting. Navigating past them slowed him down and by the time he caught up, Emma was standing in front of the paint sample display.

He held back, partly because there was no point interrupting her creative thought process but also because he was curious.

Curiosity quickly shifted to mild panic as the girl went on to pick out so many paint swatches, he gave up counting at twenty. If she used all those in his house, it would come out looking like a colorblind kid's playground. Not exactly the look he hired her for.

• • • ● ● • ● ● • • •

Emma decided to go from room to room and pray in each one. She craved inspiration, but more than inspiration, she longed for Divine fingerprints on her work.

Something told her that keeping Mr. Benedict Holmes happy was a task that bordered on impossible. The only thing she could do was rely on Heavenly guidance to create something close to the vision he had.

The first step was to ask.

She took her paint swatches and a pen and went to the first room on the top level of the house, a living room. Nope. Downstairs, maybe.

She walked downstairs, all the while keeping her heart open to hearing from Heaven. As her foot touched the last step, her heart began to pound.

Now she was on the right track.

She ran her fingers along the wall as she walked. She came to the door that led to the terrarium. The only way she could describe it was that it felt *right*. The terrarium had seemed locked on their first visit, and since moving here, she'd never given it another thought. Until now.

Her hand slid to the handle with blood rushing through her ears so loudly, she couldn't hear a thing.

Holding her breath, she pulled it downwards. The door didn't budge. Maybe it was stuck? She braced herself and tried again. Not even the slightest budge. She dropped to check the keyhole but couldn't see anything obstructing the hole.

God, am I on the right track?

She tried the handle one more time, then slid her phone out of her pocket and messaged Benedict. This was most definitely the door that made her heart pound. Yet she couldn't get in. Maybe there was more to this house than she knew.

• • • • ● • ● ● • • •

Benedict ended the call after dealing with a particularly stroppy customer. He eased the tension out of his shoulders and felt a dull ache set in behind his eyes. He knew this type of headache. It would only get worse until he got out into the fresh air.

His phone beeped and there was a message from Emma.

Emma: There's a door that won't open in the house. Can I call someone in to fix it?

Quick panic flitted through him. Calm down, man. It might not even be the cellar she's trying to get into.

Benedict: I'll see to it at my next site visit.

He hit send and hoped he was doing the right thing by trusting this girl. There were things in the cellar that weren't for her eyes. Hopefully, this was just a door to a walk-in closet or something.

Regardless, he'd have to get into the cellar as soon as possible and clear it all out *before* the girl's curiosity got the better of her.

Chapter Eight

Emma found herself glaring at the locked doors each time she walked past. She didn't like mysteries she wasn't allowed to try and solve and now she had two of them under the same roof. A sneaky thought occurred to her as well, what if some crime had been committed there?

What if?

You never really knew things like that. The police could swoop in and arrest her thinking she'd done the dirty deed. Emma's sense of style just didn't reconcile itself with prison-uniform-orange.

This wouldn't do. Benedict had said he'd sort it out and he simply hadn't been back to the house since then. She was going to have to tackle the man about coming to sort it out so she could get in. After all, he'd hired her to make the house look new again. It wouldn't do to leave the main feature all ugly and untouched.

The sooner he fixed it for her, the sooner she could start the process of restoration.

She made her way to rock painting with her mind busy on all the things that could be hidden and growing behind that door. The ladies were already busy with their rocks when she arrived.

"Hey, Emma. Don't forget, we're planting on Saturday." Vicky grinned at her which made her dimples appear.

Rock planting was not Emma's favorite part of the process, but she was never one to shrink back from all aspects of a job. Even those that involved trekking around town subversively hiding rocks.

Vicky pointed at a splodge of blue paint on Emma's shirt. "Have you been cheating on us?"

"Ah man, I liked this shirt." Emma pulled it away from her skin to see how big the mark was.

"That's what you get for cheating." Vicky was poking fun at her.

"I'm not cheating, just earning a living." Emma tried to brush off her question, but Vicky was not that easily put off.

"Seriously though, how have you been, Emma? The last we heard was that you had a client that wanted to dodge paying your account. Then you left here in a snazzy car with Mr. McHunk. What are you not telling us?"

Brenda folded her arms, paintbrush poking out from her fingers like a lone chopstick. "We all know that Mr. McHunk is none other than Benedict Holmes, one of Greyville's most eligible, though elusive, bachelors. Are you about to change that status, Emma?"

Emma resisted the urge to run and stopped herself short of glaring at the woman. If she had to come up with paint swatch color names for Brenda, they'd be various shades of dirty colors and have names like Meddling Mud Brown or Sewer Gossip Gray. That was a bit mean. *Sorry, Brenda.*

A quiet thought blossomed in her mind. What if she used this moment to find out more about the man?

"You know, Brenda," she put on her sweetest smile, "you seem to know more about Holmes than I do. I'll admit, I am quite fascinated. What can you tell me?" It wasn't hard to fake interest. Her only hope was that it didn't all backfire.

Brenda slid forward in her seat and switched modes. It was as if she had a *hot gossip* setting and Emma had found the switch.

"Oh, I called it. I could see it all over you." Brenda smirked and allowed herself a little wallow in her cleverness. "So, Benedict Holmes is quite a mystery man. What do you do for him again?"

"I'm overseeing the renovation of a house. I imagine he makes his spare cash by house flipping." Emma leaned forward as if hanging on Brenda's next words. Truth was, she didn't want to be the one talking. Not about Benedict Holmes or what he got up to.

"Right. Here's the thing though. He buys and fixes up houses, but none of those houses ever make it to the market. I know because property watching is a hobby of mine. I like knowing what's for sale and predicting which ones will sell fast. I'm pretty good at calling those that won't sell. I've said that about some houses and they've been on the market forever"

Kerry was nodding. "It's true. He bought the place next to where my mom stayed and fixed it up. There's a lady and her children living there, but it never went onto the property market."

Brenda pointed at Kerry, her finger shook with excitement. "You see? There it is. One house could maybe be for his family. But one a month? No, there's something else going on here." She paused for dramatic effect. "Maybe he's a *drug dealer*."

Vicky was frowning in concentration as she painted eyelashes onto her piglet rock. "I don't think that's how drug dealing works."

Brenda shot a frown at her. "Well, whatever he's up to, it's kept very hush-hush. Either the man is doing some seriously dodgy things, or he's secretly some legit guardian angel type. Either way," she regarded Emma with something close to sympathy, "I'd be careful around him, hon."

Emma's phone buzzed and she checked it to dodge the intensity of Brenda's conversation. It was a message from Benedict. His ears must have been burning from their conversation.

Benedict: I'm booking you for a work function tomorrow night. Suitable attire will be delivered to the house. Be ready by 7 p.m.

Brenda had read the message over her shoulder but showed no remorse. Instead, she patted Emma on the shoulder and shook her head, mouthing the words *be careful*.

• • • ● • ● • • •

Benedict sat in his usual spot at the yacht club, drinking his usual drink, but his usually quiet sanctuary was overrun with people. He didn't *hate* fundraising events, but fundraising for a secret organization had its challenges.

There was nothing upfront here, but rather a careful dance to identify potential sources of funding. New donors were brought onboard into careful tiers of the level of information they'd be privy to. It was a masterpiece of public relations that helped those who needed it while keeping their identities completely secret. In many cases, their lives depended on it. It was a tricky balance, but it worked.

Bringing Emma had been another gamble. He glanced across the room and found her completely at home chatting to one of the leading property traders in town. Benedict had been watching the man for months now, figuring out his character and deciding whether he'd be a good fit.

Emma was breathtaking in the shimmery purple floor-length dress he'd ordered for her. Her hair was clipped up, with soft curls trailing down her neck.

She turned and caught his eye, motioning for him to come closer, then gracing her company with a dazzling smile.

He looked up to find Valentino discreetly *hovering*.

He only spoke when Benedict acknowledged him with a finger salute. "Pardon me, sir. Your lady friend asked me to let you know that she requires the services of a knight."

Through all the years Benedict had been a member of the club, Valentino had been a part of the establishment. At first, Benedict had dismissed him as just another hired help, but over the years, the man had proved to be a steady source of wisdom that was always offered discreetly, never in a way that was pushy or presumptuous.

"I'm assuming you know what that means?" Valentino was suppressing a smile, Benedict could tell by the sparkle in his eyes.

"A knight in shining armor. I think she's keen to be rescued from her current company." Benedict tilted his head to study the situation. "What do you think?"

Valentino leaned closer and whispered conspiratorially, "The gentlemen was giving her a thorough introduction to the growth of his empire, one year at a time. When I left, they'd just concluded the 90's. He's taken quite a shine to her. I'd say she needs rescuing."

"Right. Let me get on that." Benedict winked at his friend and crossed the room to slip an arm possessively around Emma's waist.

She leaned closer and graced him with a dazzling smile that seemed largely cultivated to send signals and squash any ideas the older man might be entertaining, yet underneath it, Benedict sensed genuine gratitude.

• • • • ● • ● ● • • •

Emma eyeballed herself in the ladies' room mirror at the gym. She was trying to persuade herself that she could afford to take the time out to be here. Things at the house needed to move faster. But this was a good way to reduce stress and that would help her be more productive when she got back home.

At least that's what she told herself.

Her intention was to spend a few minutes on the stationary bike to get in her cardio for the day. She'd tied her hair back when none other than cancelled-wedding-Daniella came in. Emma panicked and stepped into a shower cubicle, shutting the door behind her.

"Excuse me! This one is taken."

She shot a glance at a strange lady who was desperately hiding behind her towel.

Emma closed her eyes and whispered, "Sorry! I'm hiding."

"Go hide somewhere else!" The lady's voice was shrill and loud.

Emma watched the pink-clad blurry figure pass by her stolen cubicle, muttered another quick apology, and slipped out to follow. Without thinking it through, she followed Daniella and her friend into the spinning class.

The room was painted in dark colors, with a sparkly disco ball hanging from the center of the low ceiling. Bright lights cycled through colors, making patterns on the floor and ceiling. Music pumped through the sound system, the kind of rhythm that made your heart rate speed up before you even started exercising.

Daniella and her friend chose bicycles at the front, hung their towels over the handlebars and slipped twin water bottles into the holders.

Emma had never done a spinning class before, but hey! She may just pick up some ammo.

She dubiously mounted a bike directly behind them and flinched as the wiry instructor in camo Lycra walked into the room.

For the next hour, Emma sweated and cycled, sometimes pretending to tweak the resistance knob on the bicycle when the maniac up front shouted, "Up the resistance, everybody!"

As the music faded, Emma nearly fell off the bike to keep up with Daniella and her friend. They strode along easily and Emma limped behind them trying to look natural.

Snippets of conversation drifted back to her.

"I know this is an awkward question, but what should I do with my bridesmaid dress?" Daniella's friend asked. Her hair was pulled back into a tight, black, ponytail that was as skinny as she was.

"Keep it. You can wear it to a varsity dance. Or you can sell it if you want." Daniella sounded as if she honestly couldn't care less. Emma watched her closely and saw her eyes slide sideways as she bit her lip. The girl was not as unaffected as she was pretending to be.

"No! Dani! That doesn't seem right. Are you sure you won't get back together?"

"He made it very clear that that's not what he wants. I'm sorry but I won't be volunteering for another round of that sort of bashing."

A bubble-muscled weight-lifter chose that moment to step in front of Emma. "Hey, beautiful. You must be new, I've seen it all before but never anything as fine as you."

Emma stepped sideways, trying to keep up with her targets, but bubble-boy side-stepped too.

"What's the rush? I just want to talk."

Usually, she'd turn back or head around the obstacle in another direction, but her targets were nearly out of earshot and this lump of muscle was in her way.

"Well, I don't want to talk. Step aside." She flat-stared him up and down, with the iciest non-glare she could muster.

He backed off and waved her past shaking his head at her painfully obvious lack of good taste.

She scuttled closer to Daniella and her friend, as quick as she dared without looking obvious, just in time to hear the friend invite Daniella out.

"There's this thing at the Bushwillow Club tonight. You should come, just to get your mind off things."

"I don't think I'm great company right now."

Her friend was not put off so easily. "Great. I'll fetch you at seven-thirty. Wear something pretty. Oh, what am I saying, you always look pretty." They turned to retrieve their bags and Emma slipped into the group class studio to avoid being seen.

Another toned girl with ridiculously obedient muscles that looked good in Lycra greeted her with twice the enthusiasm any normal person should have. "You're just in time for class. Cross-training for life, right?!"

"Oh no! I'm just looking for someone." Emma made a great show of looking at the other participants and shrugging in disappointment.

Toned girl and her muscles weren't put off that easily. "I understand, trust me. We all started out a little scared, hey guys?" There was a lot of head nodding and murmuring among the class. If toned girl smiled any wider, the top of her head may just fall off backward. "You'll love it, I promise."

With that, she dragged Emma the last half-meter into class and shut the door.

Dodging bubble-boy had used up Emma's last smidge of confrontation energy. She gave a weak fist pump and made her reluctant way to station one.

• • • • • • • • • •

Emma sat outside the Bushwillow Club, stifled a yawn, and questioned her sanity. Was she taking this all too far? Probably.

But she was here now and if her two targets pitched up, she was committed to following them in.

The club was a glorified community hall that morphed into whatever it was hired for. It sat like a stubborn piece of driftwood across the road from the local beach which made it popular for birthday parties, weddings, and whatever else people dreamt up for it.

With that chameleon background, Emma had no idea what she was in for. The ocean rolled restlessly next to her, waves lazily breaking then retreating as if they were shy.

This was a bad idea. Maybe she should go for a long walk on the soft sand, maybe get her feet wet, then head home to find something to eat.

Her body ached from the spinning class and she suspected she'd tweaked a muscle in her backside during the torture of the unintended cross-training session after that. Maybe she'd skip the club and head straight home. Wait! There they were.

Daniella looked pretty in white denim pants and a soft chiffon top in a shade of olive that suited her skin. Her friend wore skin-tight black and four times the amount of make-up that she actually needed.

Emma watched them pay and go in before slipping in to join the queue. She handed over her entrance fee while craning her neck to see where the girls had gone. The lighting inside the hall was muted to the same level as an uptown restaurant—not too dim to see what was on your plate, but soft enough to be kind to the person sitting across from you.

The ticket girl handed her a clipboard and pen. "Your seat number is over here. Remember to stay put." The girl winked at her and turned to take money from the next person.

Emma tucked the clipboard under her arm and walked into a hall decked out with tables and chairs. The entire floor was covered this way which ruled out a dance party. The hall was filling up and it took some time before she picked out Daniella and her friend. Daniella was whispering furiously, the poor girl didn't look happy at all.

Her friend was nodding somewhat patronizingly in a way that made Emma wonder whether she was such a good friend. What were they all here for anyway?

She opened up the clipboard to a score sheet. Her eyes flicked to the top of the page. Printed across the top in bold letters were words that filled Emma with instant regret.

Welcome to the Bushwillow Speed Dating night.

Oh no.

Chapter Nine

THE POSSIBILITY OF GETTING closer to Daniella to figure out what was going on wasn't worth this. She turned to leave but she was too late. The doors shut and some official-looking person guided the ladies to find their seats.

She checked her number and obediently sat, feeling a little light-headed. *Focus, Emma.* Stick to the mission. First, find the target. She glanced to her left trying to be as discreet as possible. Nothing. She checked to the right. Her eyes slid down the rows of women, all dressed up. Some looked hopeful, others bored and in the rest, she recognized what she was feeling. Sheer terror.

Her glance slid next to her and she nearly jumped. Daniella was right next to her. Daniella caught her eye and shook her head with an eye roll. "It looks like you want to be here about as much as I do. Were you dragged here too?"

Emma was meant to be spying, gathering intel. *Not* chatting like old friends. She nodded in what she hoped was a conspiratorial fashion and was saved from having to answer by a clear bell that rang upfront.

Her belly flipped and she opened up her folder.

"Welcome, ladies. In a few minutes, we'll be letting the gentlemen in and tonight's speed dating event will begin. You will have five minutes with each man. Stay in your seats and the men will move. Use your clipboard to note any of the men that you'd be keen to trade numbers with. You will only receive contact details if both of you chose the other. Any questions?"

The man spoke as quickly as an auctioneer and Emma found herself waiting for the noisy bang of the gavel. It never came. Instead, the bell rang again and the doors swung open.

As the room filled with testosterone, Emma fought the urge to bolt. Only twenty-five dates between her and freedom. She intended to use every one of those to get to the bottom of the split.

The chair opposite her scraped the floor as a big guy dressed in a hand-knitted reindeer sweater settled in opposite her. His round face beamed, head bobbing as if he'd decided she was the one.

"Hey, gorgeous. I think I've found the one. You must be the most beautiful girl in this place. What do you say we blow this joint and get on with our own forever?"

Emma grimaced and pointed to his sweater. "Your mom knits."

He pulled on it as if he'd forgotten he was wearing it. "Oh no, she doesn't. I picked this out from a bargain shop." He leaned forward, whispering, "I read up on all this. Psychology says women prefer a homely guy and not," his eyes slid to the jean-clad, open-necked shirt sitting across from Daniella, "someone who dressed up for the occasion."

"Oh, right." Emma couldn't help thinking she should put him straight, but that was not her mission. Her ears stretched to the conversation to the right where Danielle was dodging questions from the jeans-and-shirt guy.

Reindeer boy was a talker and Emma found it easy enough to nod and make the right noises without actually taking in a single word.

The bell rang and the next date wasn't so simple.

He was a quiet boy with eyes that slid sideways as if he would rather date the table than Emma. She needed to get him talking so she could focus on Daniella.

"Are you a *Whovian*?"

The shy boy's eyes lit up. "You're into the Doctor? Far out."

It took a single nod from Emma to set him off. Her eyes glazed over as he launched into a thick debate with himself over whether Matt, David, or Jodie did the role justice.

Danielle's current date had just finished telling her how beautiful her body was and commenting on 'how much she must work out.'

He was not high on the EQ scale because her arms crossed her chest. She didn't seem to be interested in some bozo who couldn't make eye contact and listen to what she had to say.

The bell rang, cutting off the *Whovian* halfway through his revelation of the actual meaning behind some obscure episode that Emma had never watched, though he assumed she had.

The next few were all talkers. Emma glued on a nodding smile while her ears flapped at what was happening next to her.

Reindeer jersey had reached Danielle. "Hey, gorgeous. I think I've found the one. You must be the most beautiful girl in this place. What do you say we blow this joint and get on with our own forever."

Emma cringed on his behalf. How original.

Daniella looked ready to bolt.

Reindeer boy seemed to set aside his pretense and the next question sounded sincere. "Honestly, all flirting aside. I can't believe you haven't been snatched up yet. Are you sure you're not on the rebound or something?"

Danielle blinked back tears. "I used to believe I knew what love is, but I don't know."

"Oh honey, I can help with that."

It took all Emma's self-control not to go yell at him for being insensitive. Saved by the bell. Reindeer boy moved on and Emma relaxed on Danielle's behalf.

Someone slid into the chair opposite her and she looked up with a start. "Benedict! What are you doing here?"

"The same thing you are. Speed dating." His voice was dry and it gave her the feeling he was laughing at her.

"Well, at least it's only five minutes." She put her pen down on the table and her hand brushed his. Her fingers tingled but she forced herself to leave her hand right there. His fingers lingered too and Emma wanted to scream.

"Five minutes can feel like an eternity, depending on the company."

She leaned forward and whispered furiously, "Are you spying on Daniella?"

He leaned close enough to whisper in her ear, "Are you? You do remember that that would be tip-toeing on the edges of breach of contract."

She had to distract the man. "Don't be daft." She checked her watch, crossed her arms, and looked him in the eye. "So. You've got four minutes and fifteen seconds left. Impress me."

"You want to play this game? Fine. So let me guess. Your favorite date would be a barefoot picnic on the beach, followed by a lazy swim. You like going for long drives by moonlight and your favorite spot is that cliff top in Morgan Bay where the waves crash like thunder. You like simple food, and simple pleasures like freshly picked flowers. Butterflies delight your soul. You sometimes eat a handful of berries for breakfast."

She forced her face to remain deadpan. How did he know? "Not even close."

His eyes narrowed a fraction, the only sign that he didn't believe her. "Your turn."

"What? Your favorite date?" Emma was scrambling to make the time go faster. This was beyond awkward.

"Mm. Start there. I'm waiting." He sat watching her, with his dark eyes smoldering with an emotion she couldn't put a name to.

Maybe it would be easier to discuss Dani and her tattered love life. Emma's thoughts scrambled. "I don't think you have time for dates. With you, it's all business and ruining other people's happiness."

He flinched at that as the bell rung. Emma felt hollow, scraped out. How many more of these until this nightmare was over?

The next man to occupy the space opposite her was jittery enough to make the table jiggle with his incessant knee bouncing. She was too rattled from her run-in with Benedict to face the guy. The chair next to her scraped.

"Thomas?" Daniella asked, horrified. "What are you doing here? Our rings aren't even cold yet."

"I could ask you the same thing."

Emma's head shot up so fast, she nearly gave herself whiplash. She stared from one to the other as the penny dropped.

Thomas turned to her, emotions nailed down though it took one look at his face to see that he was losing the battle. The red blotches on his neck were a dead giveaway.

His eyes were bright and slightly manic. "So tell me all about yourself."

Before Emma could answer, words came out of him as if seeing Daniella had sliced open a tender wound.

"Me?" He glanced at his brother's back. Benedict was sitting directly behind Emma, close enough to bump into him if she moved an inch.

Thomas was avoiding looking in Dani's direction, he seemed to be struggling to breathe.

Emma could see how heartbroken he was. His words didn't match his eyes. "Are you happy to be here? You can leave if you want, you know that, right?"

Thomas wasn't listening. He shook his head and muttered under his breath. Emma couldn't help wondering why these two had split up.

She leaned close and whispered, "Do you want to tell me what happened? I'm a good listener."

He stared at her as if seeing her for the first time. "I'm sorry, who are you?"

"Literally no-one. I was just wondering what happened to you that hurt you so badly. You seem to be in a lot of pain."

"It doesn't matter." his gaze slid over to his ex, "What bothers me most is who I hurt along the way. That's the killer."

Daniella threw her hand up in the face of the guy sitting opposite her. "I'm sorry, give me one moment." She turned to Thomas, bristling, "Why are you here? First, you back out of our wedding. Now you show up here and make it impossible for me to move on. What do you want from me?"

Daniella's current date stood up with his hands in his hair. "Wait. This isn't right. You two are cheating. This is for singles. I'm calling the organizers." He stuck his hand in the air waving as if he'd just discovered his feet were on hire.

Emma saw Daniella crumble as she sat in the maelstrom of chaos. Poor girl. Emma jumped up and grabbed his hand. "Hi, sorry what's your name? Patrick? Okay, Patrick. Let's not be hasty. There's more going on here than what you think. Just take a moment and breathe."

Emma's voice had a calming effect on the man and he nodded.

"That's good. I'm sure you've already met some lovely ladies tonight, yes? You don't need to blow this up over one complication."

The bell dinged and Thomas moved to the next seat, his face set in a grim mask of barely veiled pain.

Daniella shot her a grateful look. The poor girl was distraught, yet leaving would cause a scene. Emma understood the conundrum all too well. They both suffered through a few more rounds and then it was over. An official person came and fetched all their clipboards.

"Gentlemen, please take your leave of the ladies and go wait in the room next door. Ladies, we've set up refreshments for you in the corner. Please go help yourselves."

Emma bolted for the ladies' room. This date had taken more out of her than she realized. She shut herself in a booth and rested her head on the back of the door.

Someone was sobbing in the booth next to her.

Chapter Ten

EMMA WRESTLED WITH HERSELF. She wanted to go home and get out of these clothes and wash away this night.

But it wasn't in her to ignore someone in need. She tapped on the door gently. "Is everything alright in there?"

A loud sniff, then a broken voice. "I'm fine." It was Daniella.

"Okay then." No help wanted. You can't force someone to accept your offer. Emma was washing her hands and splashing water on her face when the door swung back.

Daniella had been sobbing hard. Her make-up made two panda rings around her eyes. She faced herself in the mirror, her chest still wracked with shudders from sobbing. "I don't want to go out there."

"Excuse me?" Emma squirmed in the face of the poor girl's pain.

Daniella laughed, a cold, dry sound. "My fiancé, ex-fiancé I should say, and his boorish big brother are out there. I can't face them. I don't know what to do."

"Where's the friend you came with?"

"She messaged me to say she's leaving with one of the guys she met here. So it's just me." She groaned into her hands.

Emma thought it through for a split second, then shrugged out of her coat. If she was in Dani's predicament, she'd climb out the window and be gone in a few seconds but she somehow didn't think this girl would cope with that. "Here, put this on. We're going to get you out of here."

Daniella blinked, studied Emma's face for a moment, then asked, "How, though?"

Emma grinned at her and pulled the hood of the jacket over Daniella's head. Warmth flooded through her for this girl she barely knew. It was almost like she could feel Heaven smiling. "I've got a plan. Come on."

Together they snuck out the door, turned right instead of left, and found themselves in the kitchen. One whispered conversation later, Emma and Daniella were led out the back door by none other than the head chef himself.

"Stay safe, ladies. Go quickly before the others start leaving."

They crept down a dark alleyway towards the front of the building, scanned left and right, and ran across the open section to where Emma's car was parked. She pressed the button to unlock, checked the area again to make sure nobody was coming, then they both threw themselves into the car and shut the doors.

Daniella craned her neck. "They're coming out. Drive!"

Emma turned the key and pulled out into the empty street just as Benedict walked out of the building.

Safely out of sight, Dani sank into her chair, cradled her head, and shook hard.

Emma thought she was crying and was scrambling for soothing things to say, but then a laugh erupted from the girl. They caught eyes and laughed again, feeling the release of stress.

They'd left the hall far behind when Daniella turned to Emma. "I just made myself your problem. Sorry about that."

"Are you kidding? That was the most fun I had all night."

Daniella pulled a wry face. "If we're honest, the standard wasn't exactly set very high. Just drop me off here, I can walk home."

Emma chuckled, this girl was delightful. "I'd rather drop you safely at your front door if it's all the same with you?"

"Bentley Heights, do you know the apartments? I'm Dani, by the way."

"I do actually. I used to have a friend that lived there." She took the next right and started weaving. "Emma. Nice to meet you."

They pulled up outside Dani's building and Emma blurted out, "The way your friend ditched you, does that happen a lot?"

"I nearly said no, but thinking about it, yes. She does do that. Normally I'd take it in my stride, but—" She swallowed hard and looked away.

Emma blinked away the image of soggy, unfinished wedding invitations. "Some days, you're just not in the mood. I get that."

Dani shot her a grateful glance for not having to finish her sentence. "Now that I think about it, you've been a better friend to me and I've known you for a few minutes."

A tiny little thought tiptoed lightly through Emma. This was all too easy. "Do you like painting?"

• • • ● • ● • • •

"Bro, that speed dating was a terrible idea. Why did you suggest it?" Thomas spread thick peanut butter on his toast. Morning light gleamed on the polished marble top.

Benedict popped the toaster and reached for honey. "Firstly, peanut butter is not for breakfast." He shook his head at his little brother as if he were three years old. He spread a thick layer of honey on his toast and bit off a piece to give himself time to word his answer right.

"Someone at the office gave me tickets. I thought it might be good for you to chat with some other ladies. You know, get a glimpse of what else is out there."

Thomas brushed crumbs off his fingers. "The dust hasn't even settled on my broken engagement, yet you want me to see what else is available. What is wrong with you?"

"Need I remind you that Daniella saw fit to be out and about meeting new men too?"

"That's beside the point."

Benedict towered over his brother. "No, that's where you are wrong. She has already moved on. You need to let her go."

Thomas slammed his half-eaten toast onto the plate. He stood too, eyeball to eyeball with Benedict. "Stop. Just stop." He picked up his car keys and stormed out.

Benedict watched him go while swallowing the last of his toast and honey. With a shrug, he picked up the peanut butter toast and ate that too.

Who knew? The kid was right, it was good. He brushed crumbs off his fingers and checked his phone. Nothing from the office.

Last night had confirmed a problem for him. He'd seen Emma getting awfully buddy-buddy with Dani. He couldn't afford to let that happen. It would seem that his plan to keep her so occupied with the house wasn't enough.

He dialed the office. "Liz, I won't be in today. I have a little matter I need to take care of."

• • • • ● • ● • • •

Emma walked past the locked cellar door and doubled back. She just couldn't get it out of her head. What could be important enough to be locked away like this? Unless the family heirlooms were locked up in there, or it was a crime scene.

The terrarium was different, it might not even be locked, just rusted shut. This cellar, though? She shuddered. Living above a potential crime scene wasn't a thought she relished. Bending down low she peered through the keyhole but all she could see was her mashed up eyelashes and a nondescript curtain.

Off-limits or not, she was going to get in there.

Not today, of course.

But soon. Maybe after she'd been to the shop to buy milk and things she needed to bake an apple pie. It was her turn to bake for the rock painting group that night and Dani would be coming for the first time.

Emma grinned at the thought. Making friends with this girl was easier than she'd been expecting. That thought made her stop for a moment.

Was she doing this for the right reasons?

"God, I want what You want. I feel like they're right for each other. Am I being manipulative?"

Her words tripped off her lips and died at her feet. Silence met her question.

"Nice chat, thanks, God." She flinched at being cheeky with Him, and whispered a quiet, "Sorry about that."

Initially, it had been about the money. That shifted when the big deposit landed in her account. Now?

She had felt strongly that Thomas and Dani belonged together. But then Benedict had to go poking his nose around, and now—if she were honest—it was also about getting under his skin. Or was it?

"Mr. Benedict bit off more than he could chew when he decided to mess with me."

But was that fair on Thomas and Dani?

Emma groaned and rubbed her temples to make the pain go away. "God, things would be so much easier if you could pull on a skin suit and come down here and chat to me."

She didn't expect an answer to her question instantly, so she settled on heading to the shops before she could start obsessing over this closed door again. Shops first, then some further sleuthing. Pulling her handbag over her shoulder, she checked the time and headed out the door.

Chapter Eleven

EMMA TRIED TO SHAKE the sense of unease she felt as she unlocked the door to Benedict's house and let herself in. After her shop run, she found herself avoiding heading back to the house.

Don't be silly, girl. This house is only temporary, you won't be staying on. Of course, it's not going to feel comfortable.

She rolled her shoulders a few times to try and shake off the tension. What she wouldn't give to feel safe. Right now, she had more money in the bank than she'd seen in years, but it wasn't helping her feel safe at all. Hmm, so much for that.

But first, she had a pie to bake.

Emma didn't like cooking much, but she was a self-confessed stress-baker. Anytime she found her worries piling up, she'd bake and work her frustration into whatever dough she was kneading at the time.

Her hands moved on autopilot as she rolled out the dough, peeled and sautéed apples, and greased the pie dish. Assembling it all didn't take long, even though she created the lid from woven strips of dough. She gave the pie a quick brush with beaten egg to give it a golden gleam and it was ready to be baked.

Heat from the oven washed over her as she swung the door and popped the pie on the rack. She shut the door and set the timer. Patience.

It took patience to be a good baker. She had forty-five minutes to kill.

Maybe pruning roses would help. A neglected garden grew next to the house with an abundance of rose bushes that looked like they could do with some TLC. She headed straight for them with shears in hand.

The bushes were a mangled mess of branches that grew in many directions, covered in dead buds. She knew about pruning from her dad and set to work on the first one.

"Sorry bush, this is going to feel cruel. I know what I'm doing, so trust me, okay?"

With a quick adjustment to her gardening gloves, she got to work on the first one. It took a good twenty minutes to get off all the dead weight that was stopping the bush from thriving.

The pile of dead branches grew as she methodically worked her way from bush to bush. One stood in a particularly windy part of the garden, its stem was covered in thorns. "Oh, you poor thing. Life has been rough for you."

She trimmed that one back extra far before standing back to admire her work.

"What is going on here?"

Benedict was back. Heat flooded her cheeks at the thought of seeing him last night.

"What does it look like I'm doing?"

"I liked these." He waved at the shorn-down stump of a rosebush. "Why are you killing them?" There was an edge to his voice.

Emma forced herself to breathe and not let the words rush out in a panic-induced high-pitched squeak. Keeping her voice low, she asked, "Don't you know how pruning works?"

"Pruning? This is a massacre."

Emma bristled at the man's ignorance as her phone alarm beeped in her back pocket. "Pie. Do you want some?" Anything to get him out of the garden so he can stop complaining. She watched his face shift.

"What kind of pie?"

"Apple and cinnamon." She'd baked it for the stones crew later on, but sacrificing it now was a small price to pay. "Follow me."

The timer on the oven buzzed as she walked into the kitchen. She lifted the pie out and placed it on a rack to cool a bit before cutting into it.

"Tea?"

Benedict slid into the chair sniffing the air. "Did you bake that from scratch?"

"I did." It took less than a minute to make two cups of tea. She took cream out of the fridge, cut two pieces, and spooned cream on top. She slid Benedict's pie and tea across the table to him and watched as he took a spoonful, place it in his mouth, and visibly melted.

"This is so good."

"So about the locked room. Do you have any idea what's behind the door?" She grinned at him, she couldn't help herself. Maybe she'd get somewhere if she caught him off-guard.

His face stayed blissful, but he shot a flat hand and mumbled, "Mm-mm."

"What could be so bad that you won't tell me?"

A message came through on Benedict's phone and hardness set into his jawline as he scanned the contents.

"I'm sorry, I have to go."

"But what about the room?"

He ignored her question as he scooped up his keys. "I'll see you later for dinner."

• • • • ● • ● • • •

Emma led the way upstairs to the rock painting studio. Dani trailed behind her with her gaunt cheeks and the frown on her forehead which seemed to have become a part of her personality. They were the first ones to arrive, which gave them time to settle in.

Only once they sat down next to each other, did Emma feel a stab of doubt.

Dani took it all in with her hands folded on her lap. "What are we doing here?"

Emma stumbled over explaining the concept. It made perfect sense in her head, but saying it out loud made it all sound a bit loony. "We paint rocks, then we hide them in the city for people to find."

Dani wasn't convinced. "Why?"

Emma spread her up-turned palms but was saved from having to explain by the noisy arrival of the ladies. They clattered upstairs laughing and chatting already.

Vicky and Kerry were deep in conversation about nappies and how often they needed to be changed. Brenda came straight over and shoved her hand under Dani's nose.

"Brenda. And you are?"

As Dani reached out to shake the woman's hand, Emma said, "This is Dani. She needs a new hobby and potentially new friends. So be nice, Brenda."

Brenda flicked her eyes over Emma wordlessly before taking her seat.

Emma rolled her eyes at Dani. "Don't mind her, she's just like that. Here, pick out a rock that you like." She held the rock bowl closer to Dani.

Dani's choice of rock was so small, it fitted neatly in the palm of her hand.

"Are you good with fine details?"

"Oh, not really. You're right. I should probably start with something bigger." Dani took a hefty one, still frowning. "I can paint anything?"

Emma nodded. "Yep. When I don't know what to paint, I pick out colors that feel right. From there it usually comes together."

Dani took a deep breath and reached for a tub of white and a tub of black paint.

Emma noticed but said nothing. Monochrome could be pretty too. For her rock, she picked out light pink, darker fuchsia, and two shades of green. She was feeling spring blossoms. For what she had in mind, she picked out three skinnier brushes.

She held out the brush holder to Dani who picked out one large one and one so tiny, it could paint dust specks. The ladies all settled in and a quiet buzz on conversation settled over the room.

"Now we paint." Emma sketched her blossoms onto her rock before starting. Once she had a layout she liked, she coated the whole thing in a thin layer of white. Her pencil marks still showed through, just as she'd hoped.

With deft dabs, half her rock was soon covered in cheerful blossoms. She set it aside to dry before adding the leaf details.

Emma was painting a slow, deliberate line of black across her rock, working from the bottom up. The black paint she was using gleamed thickly in the light. When she got halfway, she got a new brush and start overlaying the white onto the black. It smeared, blended, and came out a smooth gray.

Her technique was great, even though the results were rather somber.

She kept going until the white paint left the black paint behind. There was something poetic and heartbreaking in the way she approached her artwork.

With the background all covered up by deep black fading to lighter shades of gray. She sighed as she set it aside to dry. The rock seemed to reflect all the unspoken emotion in her stormy eyes.

Kerry glanced across the table at Dani's freshly painted rock. "You've got a good technique. Are you a painter?"

Dani kept her eyes on her rock and shook her head. She had the skinny brush in her hand and had loaded it up with black paint.

Emma saw Kerry's wide eyes slide sideways in an unspoken question. *Is she okay?*

Emma shook her head and they shared a conspiratorial wordless cringe. The girl was not okay. Using the tiny paintbrush in her hand she traced out the naked branches of a barren tree. No leaves, no flowers, just a stark stem, and branches poking out in awkward directions.

She finished the crooked tree, rinsed her brush, and folded her hands in her lap. "Now what?"

• • • ● • ● • ● • • •

Benedict read the email while his mind churned in three different directions. The family described in the email was a single mom and her three children. All boys.

Some placements were easy and took no extra thought. This one, however, struck close to home. More than anything, he wanted this family safe and happy. He ran through the places he'd recently acquired that might be suitable.

He opened up the list and scrolled down. *Show me, God.* Where do you want this family? One of the older houses caught his eye. A wooden house right on the beach. He checked the ages of the boys. Sure enough, there was a school not far from where they'd be.

He shut his eyes and for a moment, he could see them. Three little boys running barefoot on the sand, laughing with the wind in their hair, while their mom watched from the porch where she sat sipping iced tea.

This was the one.

The distances he was going to have to cover were significant. It meant he'd be running a mercy mission tonight.

Emma was penciled in for a working supper, but there was nothing urgent there. The girl was nicely on schedule.

There was only one thing for it. Cancel Emma, don his imaginary Knight in shining armor helmet and go fetch this family before more harm could be done.

There wasn't much he could do to right the wrongs in this world, but this? This was his ground and he did it well.

He sent a text to Emma.

Chapter Twelve

EMMA GOT THE MESSAGE from Benedict canceling dinner plans and felt a sting of something she didn't care to identify. Mostly, she felt relief. Right?

Yet there was something deeply satisfying about meeting with Benedict to hammer things through and argue over whether it was better to install aluminum window frames or wood.

Irritation brewed in her chest like a hot ball of fudge sauce.

Considering the man wouldn't be coming to the house, nothing stopped her from having a look inside the locked room. If she could get in, of course.

Before her conscience could stop her, she pushed off the bed and padded downstairs barefoot. The grass was cold and wet enough to stick to her legs. It sent a shiver through her and made her itchy.

She reached the door, put her hand on the handle, took a deep breath, and pushed. The door didn't budge. Nothing she didn't expect. Step two. Keyhole.

Checking left and right, which was silly because she knew she was alone, she bent down and peered through the keyhole. At first, her eyelashes got in the way. With a bit of wiggling, she shifted them out of the way.

Gloom hung over the room behind the door. In the dim light, she could just make out the shape of a dresser. The surface was cluttered as if whoever had been in the room had just stepped out for a moment and would be coming back soon.

The keyhole just wasn't big enough for her to see anything useful.

Emma made her way to the window. Sure enough, the curtains were drawn, but the one had lifted and left enough of a gap for her to peer through.

She shoved her face right up against the glass and squinted her eyes trying to see. A vague shape of a couch, dark patches on the walls—posters?—and a cupboard door standing slightly open. Beyond that, the room and its contents remained shrouded in mystery.

It fueled her irritability instead of calming it.

"Excuse me, miss. Can I help you?" The voice came from close behind her, right in the yard.

Panic flooded through Emma and she stepped back, nearly tripping over a daisy bush. A young man dressed in camo uniform stood meters from her with his hands over his mouth and a shocked look on his face.

"Oh no. I shouldn't be speaking to you. Please don't tell Mr. Holmes."

• • • • • • • • • •

Benedict pulled up outside the house and double-checked the address in the text he'd received. All seemed quiet. It was 11 pm, and if all went to plan, they should be coming out soon. He eased the car door open trying to make as little noise as possible.

He left the driver's side open and eased the back door open silently. Crouching down, he peered through the gloom, waiting to see if there was any movement from inside the property. A rustling in the bushes around the side of the house set him on high alert.

A figure appeared from the gloom, frail and small, holding hands with two smaller bodies, both stumbled along as if not quite awake.

Benedict moved fast. He reached the pavement as the woman got close.

She held out two small hands for him to take and whispered, "I have to go back for the baby."

Her eyes were wild with terror and her hands shook.

Benedict got into her line of sight, forcing her eyes to fix on his face. "You've got this. One more step. In, out. You can do it."

A deep shiver passed through the tiny woman, but grim resolve set in her mouth. She turned reluctantly and headed back into the house.

Benedict's insides squirmed at not being able to go in her place, but it was something only she could do.

He led the two sleepy boys and bundled them into the backseat where he had soft blankets waiting for them. The older one squinted at him through one half-opened eye, but Benedict grinned and whispered, "We're going on an adventure." With a finger to his lips, he winked at the young boy.

A frown brushed the boy's forehead, but then he nodded, climbed in the car, and put a protective arm over his little brother who'd gone straight back to sleep as if he didn't care what was going on.

It took seven minutes and forty seconds for the woman to appear with her baby bundled in her arms. She was shaking so badly Benedict worried that she'd drop the child.

He ushered her onto the back seat and slipped the door closed with as little noise as possible. The car rolled down the hill easily before he turned the engine to get it started. When they were a safe distance away, he fired up the engine and headed for the freeway. Hyper-vigilance pumped through his veins and by the third time he checked the rear-view mirror, the woman caught his eye.

There was a tremor in her voice. "You didn't have to do all that. I don't think he'll wake up, he's got two bottles of whisky in him."

"We follow the protocols regardless. It's how we were trained." Benedict shrugged and smiled at the woman who sat clutching her baby and her son who stared at Benedict with wide eyes as if he hadn't quite decided whether to trust him or not.

"Where are you taking us?" She fought the tremor this time and the words came out sharp.

"Safety. That's all I can say right now. It's quite a distance from here, so get some sleep if you can."

The woman bit her lips and stared out the window. He could see her face every time they drove under the pool of light from the overhead streetlights, then it would dip to black in between.

He pitched his voice low, gentle, and calm. "You've been through hell, but it's over now. I will not let any harm come to you or your boys."

Something in his tone must have got through to her. She settled back and seemed to breathe more easily.

Now to get them into their new home.

• • • ● • ● • • •

It took Emma a moment to recover from the shock of being caught in the act of snooping. Honestly? She had a right to know what was in the room, she had to live in the same house. Also, why was this young man on Benedict's property and why was he so obviously scared of the man?

"Oh hi! My name is Emma." She graced him with the kind of smile that always got her quick service at the coffee shop. "I haven't been in this house long enough to introduce myself to the neighbors. I'm so glad you, er, popped in."

The young man was still flustered and muttered at the ground while pounding his forehead half-heartedly with a fist. She shoved her hand out right under his nose.

"So nice to meet you. I didn't catch your name?" She blinked questioningly.

"Me, I'm James."

"Help me out here, James. What am I not supposed to be telling Mr. Holmes?"

James deflated more than Emma thought possible.

"I'm supposed to be invisible, I'm here to guard you. Or rather, anyone that lives in that house. I'm not meant to be spotted and

I'm most certainly not meant to speak to you. Ever. Mr. Holmes would fire me so fast."

"Why would you be guarding this house? I don't understand."

"Have you been *rescued*?" His voice dropped on the word 'rescued' as if he were whispering secrets.

"In a sense, I guess so?"

"Then I'm here to protect you." He grinned broadly, doffed his hat, and made a great show of *vanishing* into the bushes with his finger to his lips.

That was odd. Emma frowned in his direction before heading back inside. By the time she'd whipped up a batch of chocolate chip-laced brownies, she's settled on a strategy.

If Invisible James really did lurk in the greenery around this house, he might be willing to help her get into the cellar. She just had to find out what his weakness was and keep baking for him. Sooner or later, he would crumble.

Her little spider had found her and was hanging around on the ceiling in the kitchen. "Hey, Legs." She forced down a shudder and waved, determined to make peace with the little guy. Or girl? How could you tell with spiders anyway?

She'd loaded a plate with brownies to take outside for Invisible James when her phone rang. It was Kerry.

"Hey girl, we've decided to go rock planting tonight instead of Saturday. Can we come to fetch you?"

Emma slid the plate onto the table to check her watch. "What time? And why?"

"A couple of people have things that have come up on the weekend. So we figured why not tonight?" Kerry's voice dropped to a pseudo-whisper. "We're hiding things. It should be done at night."

"Can't argue with that!" Emma did a quick mental rearrange of her plans. "Okay sure, why not."

"Can Dani come? I like her."

"I'll check. I hope so, I like her too."

"Where did you find her, anyway?" Kerry had water running in the background.

"Please tell me you're getting ready to wash dishes and you're not on the loo?"

"Ask me no secrets and I'll tell you no lies." Kerry chuckled. "You were telling me about Dani. Out with it. We've been your only friends for as long as I've known you."

Emma thought it all through and decided she wasn't ready to go there. "Ask no questions and I'll tell you no lies."

"Emma!"

"I'm joking, I'm joking." She could tell some of her story safely. "We met at speed-dating. I rescued her from a guy she didn't want to hook up with."

The silence on the other side of the phone was deafening. It didn't last long. "Speed dating?! When did you go speed dating? And why didn't you invite me?"

"It was a last-minute thing. I didn't intend to go. It just kind of happened?"

"Fine, I'll forgive you this time. Next time, you'd better take me with you. Is that a deal? Oh gosh, look at the time. We're meeting at the studio and we'll walk from there. Comfy shoes, okay?"

"Yes, mom." Emma laughed at Kerry's loud sigh.

She ended the call and messaged Dani. The answer came back almost instantly.

Dani: Rock planting sounds horrible, but it's better than sitting here being lonely by myself. I'd love to come.

Emma typed a quick response and hit send. The spider took it all in without comment.

"Well, Legs. My strategy is working. Almost too well. Now all I have to do is wait for the right moment to present itself and plant some seeds."

She frowned at her buddy and wondered whether she should rather just take the little guy out to the garden. No time now, she had to get ready.

Chapter Thirteen

THE SUN WAS RISING by the time Benedict pulled up to a set of big gates. The guard recognized him and waved as he pulled to a stop.

"Morning Sir. Who have we got here?" He peered into the back of the car where Trish and the boys were all sleeping in a messy pile.

"The wooden house right on Beach Drive. Number thirty-two."

"I'll fetch the keys for you. I won't be a moment."

Trish stirred while the gatekeeper jogged off towards his brick guardhouse.

Benedict waited for her eyes to open. He saw the panic set in. "Just a little bit further now."

He saw her properly for the first time in daylight. Her black hair stood out in a wild fuzz that would need more than a good brush to tame. Underneath the dark circles and her pained expression were the hints of a beautiful woman.

Give her a few months of safe living and she'd be unrecognizable. "Come on, let's get you guys settled in."

The woman didn't budge. "I don't understand."

Benedict had seen it before, the fractured self-worth. It would seem he'd got to her at just the right time.

The guard came back and handed over a bunch of keys. "You remember which one this is?"

"Oh yes. Thanks, Earl. You're doing good work."

As he drove off, the gates clanged shut behind him with a loud *thunk*.

The oldest brother had woken up, he stared at the gates with wide eyes. "Are we in jail?"

Benedict swallowed a laugh. "No, buddy. That gate is for keeping things out." He drove the familiar roads until they crested a hill to find a vast expanse of ocean stretched out before them, glittering in the early morning sun.

"Woah! Mommy, look!"

There was enough awe in the little guy's voice to cause Benedict's eyes to water. He resisted and the moisture left obediently.

The little brother woke up and shrieked as if he'd just had the best dream and woke up to find it was real.

Three streets down and a turn to the left, they pulled up at a roaming house right on the beach.

Benedict pulled up in the drive and turned to his precious cargo. "Welcome home."

• • • ● • ● ● • • •

Emma and Dani hung out at the back of the group. They each had a small bag of rocks, Emma's were all the ones she'd painted, while Dani's contained her one rock and a few spares from other people.

They all wore head-to-toe black, the regulars had small logos on the shirts that proclaimed *Rock The City* in discreet writing on the back.

Emma shook her head at the branding. It was a little bit much, but she went along with it anyway.

They'd carefully stuck small stickers onto the bottom of each rock with the social media posting details. Dani's eyes had lit up when she'd seen that, and she'd dug out her phone and quickly found and followed the *Rock The City* accounts on all the platforms.

"So what now?" Dani was enjoying this all too much. The poor girl needed a life. Much like Emma.

"C'mon. We're heading into the park." Emma led the way and Dani soon caught up. She had to figure out how to get onto the subject of Thomas.

"I'm glad you asked me to join you. I think ... tonight would have been a horrible one to be home alone."

Emma led down a trail to the left. It was lit by gentle lamplight from overhead which shone in pools at regular intervals. Her heart sped up. This was it, her opening. *Play it cool, Emma.*

"What would you have been doing tonight?"

Dani cleared her throat and pointed at a hollow in the base of a tree. "How about there?"

"It's a good spot, go for it." *Come on girl, don't change the subject.*

Dani fished out a rock, and it happened to be hers. "It feels strangely personally leaving this here."

Emma eyed the gloomy rock, trying to keep her face from giving away her misgivings. "You don't have to leave it. You can hang onto it if you prefer."

Dani nodded stoically, then hugged her rock and quickly placed it into the hollow as if she was doing the world a big favor. "There. I did it."

"Well done. Your first one is always the hardest. By the time you've painted a couple of dozen, you'll be flinging them down as if you were sowing seed."

Dani pulled down the branches and gave her rock one last lingering look. "I sewed feeling seeds."

Emma didn't know what to say so she spun around to look for the hidey-hole. "So what would you have been doing tonight, if not having all this fun with me?"

Dani walked along next to Emma, fishing around in her bag for the next rock. "I would have been planning my honeymoon."

"Would have been. There's a whole lot of story and pain hidden in those three words. What went wrong?" Emma's heart was pounding. She was proud of how steady her voice sounded. How casual.

Dani pulled a rock out and squinted at it under the lights. On the rock was a painted heart, encircled by thorns.

"How appropriate." A dry laugh escaped her lips. "I don't know. We did try to talk about it, but he could never give me a straight answer."

"There must be something you can think of?" Emma didn't want to push the girl, but her gut told her that she needed to understand.

"Everything was fine one day. Then we got into a disagreement, it wasn't even an argument. But suddenly things turned serious and before I knew what was happening, we were both saying the words we didn't mean."

"Wedding stress can push you over the edge like that."

"We weren't stressed though. I mean, we're both pretty easygoing. Something changed, and I don't know what."

Emma felt her heartbeat still. This was her moment. "What if we could figure it out? Would you want to know?" She tucked a rock in under a hedge so the tiniest sliver of it was sticking out.

Dani sounded small and tired. "It wouldn't do much good. I think the bridges have been burned. There's no going back from where we are in our relationship now. It's completely up in flames."

"Put that out of your thinking for the moment." She snuck a glance at Dani and could see the girl wasn't interested in playing along, not yet anyway. She tried again. "Okay, how about this. Pretend I'm your fairy godmother. I can grant you any wish you want me to. Would your wish be to get back together?"

"You want to be my flying, magic-wand waving fairy godmother? Why?"

"Humor me. Just answer the question. Please."

Dani smiled sadly. There wasn't even a breath of hesitation. "Of course."

• • • • ● • ● ● • •

Benedict pulled into the driveway at 7 p.m. His brain was feeling the lack of sleep and his body was tired and cranky after driving for so long. But his heart, soul, and spirit were satisfied. Maybe it was some misguided knight in shining armor complex. Whatever it was, it worked for him.

He pushed the front door open. "Thomas! Are you here?"

Silence. That was hopeful, maybe he'd gone out. Benedict took a quick walk through the house. The kitchen was a mess of dirty cups and bowls. Not how he'd left it at all.

"Thomas! Why are you such a pig? This place is a mess." His voice echoed back to him through the silent house.

He strode through to Thomas's bedroom and shoved the closed door open. He found his brother wrapped in a duvet like a burrito. The curtains were still drawn and a stench of stale air and dirty socks lingered in the air.

"It's seven o'clock. You've been in this bed all day. Get moving, you slug."

Thomas mumbled something unintelligible and buried himself further under the duvet.

Benedict did the only thing that made sense. He fetched a bucket of icy water and tipped it.

Thomas flew up in shock, his eyes wide. They slid from Benedict to the bucket and back. His breathing was quick and hard. Without a word, he pushed past Benedict, grabbed a jacket, and headed out into the night.

Benedict let him go, quietly congratulating himself on the fire he'd managed to light under his brother's rear-end. It was about time.

He made himself a strong cup of black coffee and settled on the porch railing, waiting for Thomas to come back. His mind free-wheeled through the day, sifting through all the emotions he'd felt at getting another family settled into safety.

They didn't touch his heart but just filtered through his mind for cataloging and referring back to. Just another small reminder of why what he did was meaningful.

His coffee cup was already cold before an icy thought touched his mind. Why was Thomas not back yet? Benedict had expected him to go around the block, cool off, and come back in with the look he got on his face when Benedict pushed him too far.

He checked the time, 8:30 p.m. It wasn't late, but with no sleep the night before, he was feeling strung out as cheese on a toasted sarmie.

Growling at the thought of going out to find his brother, he knew he wouldn't rest if he didn't. Slow-burning rage fueled him beyond where his depleted energy could take him. He pulled the door shut behind himself, and jogged out in the darkness.

Chapter Fourteen

EMMA AND DANI EACH had one rock left to plant when Dani spotted someone she knew up ahead.

"I'm going to say hi. I'll catch up with you soon."

Emma was pondering where to plant her last rock and waved Dani off with an absent-minded smile. A large tree brooded over a gap in the vegetation that looked like it would make the perfect hiding place for a rock.

The one she had left was a star painted on a velvety dark background. It seemed appropriate that it would be a little harder to find than the others.

Dani was chatting happily, so Emma slipped behind the tree and found herself in a moonlit clearing. In the center of the space stood a small mound of rocks. It seemed too easy, but she could just add her painted rock to the pile. She walked around it slowly, mulling on the idea.

As she placed it close to the ground, the tree leaves rustled. She spun around expecting to see Dani, but instead, it was a tall, skinny guy who was sopping wet as if he'd been caught in a rain shower.

He dived into the opening and scooted straight in behind the hedge, staring through the gaps in the trees with wild eyes. He hadn't seen her yet, so she could study him as much as the low light allowed. He was weirdly familiar.

The man sighed and his shoulders slumped as tension drained from his body. He saw her and she watched his eyes widen as his body went stiff and a strangled grunt came from his throat.

"Hi." Emma waved in what she hoped was a friendly, not intimidating way.

"Sorry! I didn't realize anyone was in here." That voice, she recognized it from speed dating?

"Oh don't go, I'm about to leave. I've done what I came here for." Emma would have to squeeze past the guy if she intended to leave.

"Don't mind me, I'm just hiding from my maniac brother."

She *did* recognize him. It was Thomas. Was this all by chance, or did Jesus have a hand in this?

"Sure, don't let me stop you. I have to go meet a friend anyway." Emma stepped towards him, hoping he'll get the hint and leave, but he seemed too flustered. "Well, if I see any maniac brothers out there, I won't tell them you're in here."

"Thanks." He smiled at her, but it was pure lip service with nothing to back it up in his eyes. This boy was sad.

Emma pushed past him and willed Dani to come looking for her.

"What were you doing in here?" His curiosity must have got the better of his paranoia.

"I was, er, planting a rock."

He sniggered, "Why? Are you hoping it will grow into a mountain?"

"Funny. You made a joke."

"Trust me, I used to make them all the time. Nowadays, there's not too much *funny* in my world."

Emma grew completely still. The air buzzed with the electric charge of a Heavenly opportunity. "Do you want to talk about it?"

Thomas's eyes snapped back to her. "What? Oh no. There's no real point. It's a disaster that can't be fixed." He looked utterly miserable and Emma felt her heart pull.

"I don't believe that."

"Well, then you're a fool."

Emma blinked fast, not sure she was hearing right. "Excuse me?"

"You know nothing. You can't just make statements like that." His eyes dropped back to the ground. "Sorry, that was uncalled for."

Emma scrambled inside. *Lord, what must I say to this guy?* She heard her name being called, her friends were starting to wonder where she was. "I'd better get going." Half-way through the trees, she turned back. "Don't get stuck in never. Things might work out differently to how you expect them to."

"Maybe in your fairytale life. Not mine. But thanks anyway."

• • • ● • ● • • •

Benedict had checked all the places he thought he'd find his brother and still come up empty-handed. He didn't have time for this nonsense.

He'd sent half a dozen messages to common acquaintances, but they all came back saying the same thing – no sign of Thomas.

Benedict stopped running, it was time to slow down and think this through. His brother was technically a grown man, though, to Benedict, he'd always be small and need looking after.

He should just head home and give the kid some space. Maybe he'd come back with some sense in his head. Or maybe he'd taken himself back to Dani. It would be just like Thomas to undo all this hard work in a moment of weakness.

He had to message her and see.

Benedict: Hi, is Thomas with you by any chance?

It pained him to hit send. But this was the most efficient way of finding his brother, even if it meant exposing the fact that things were a little out of whack. Efficiency trumped pride.

He watched as the single tick became double and then they both turned blue. She should have been typing, but instead, he got nothing. He waited for a full five minutes, checking his phone in impatient glances. Nothing.

Dani had blue-ticked him.

Emma was struggling to focus on what her new friend was saying. The back of her mind kept churning over how she could get these two to fall over each other accidentally. It was only when Dani nearly threw her phone that Emma snapped back to the present.

"Sorry, what?"

"Benedict! He's gone and lost Thomas. I'm so frustrated with that man." Red spots of anger rode high on Dani's cheeks.

"I'm not following. What's going on?"

Dani shoved her phone at Emma for her to read the message. She nearly laughed but managed to contort it into something resembling horrified shock. It would seem that big brother wasn't as in control as he thought he was.

"Are you worried? About Thomas, I mean."

"I don't care about him anymore. Not after what he did to me."

"I'm not buying it, Dani. Who is the real problem, Thomas or his big brother?"

Dani frowned. "You know, you're right. Benedict is a big problem. He's a bossy dictator who meddles all the time. It's like he can't keep his nose out of everybody's business. But here's the problem. If Thomas truly loved me like he says he does, what Benedict says wouldn't have such power over him."

"Big brother issues. I get it."

"It's more than that. Benedict is a strange man full of secrets. I'm usually pretty good at reading people. It's one of the reasons I chose to study social work. But with him, I just don't know. I used to think he was a good guy, just misunderstood. But after what he did to me and Thomas, I'm starting to wonder about all his secrets."

They'd caught up to the others and Emma had to bite back all her curious questions. So Benedict was more of an enigma than she thought.

Why was that not a surprise?

Chapter Fifteen

EMMA DROPPED DANI AT home and made her way to the house. She pulled up on the driveway underneath the branches of the big weeping willow branch that hung too close to her car. As much as she loved the tree, she was going to have to trim it back.

A loud sniff cut through the sound of her feet crunching on the leaves and she froze. Panic flooded through her and she fought the urge to run.

Another sniff, followed by a cough. Somebody was sitting on the porch stairs in the shadows.

"Who's there?" Emma forced boldness into her words. She was tough and capable. *Don't mess with this girl.*

A lanky figure unfolded himself off the stairs and started walking towards her. Cold fear froze Emma to the spot and she couldn't move.

"I'm sorry. I'll be going. Don't let me bother you." Another loud sniff.

It was a man, his voice was familiar, yet at the same time, she just couldn't place it. He stepped into the pale glow of the porch light and recognition slid through her. It was Thomas, the cold-footed bridegroom. He was a little bit drier than when she'd seen him in the park, but his hair was still wet and he was shivering. At least he didn't pose an obvious threat.

"What are you doing here? Can I help you?"

"You're the girl from the park. I didn't know anyone was living here, I'll just go. I'm sorry."

Emma fought with herself. It would be simple to let him leave, but keeping him around might mean some inside info on his big brother. After her little chat with Dani, that could only be good.

"Don't go yet. Let's get you dry at least. Come on."

Thomas hesitated, but she held the door open and waved him inside. The aroma of fresh cheese scones wafted out the opening and it must have changed his mind as he suddenly became meek.

"Let's go, big boy. I'm Emma, by the way."

"Thomas." He held out a frozen hand on his way past that made her shiver. She had to bite her tongue from coming back with *I know*.

She threw him the biggest towel she had. "Wrap yourself in that and give me your wet shirt. I'll put the kettle on so long."

Thomas nearly tripped over a tin of paint in the hallway. The house was more of a construction site than a place to welcome guests.

"Don't mind the state of this place, we're busy renovating."

Thomas glanced around and shrugged as if it made no difference to him. It didn't take long for him to come back wrapped in a towel and looking quite sorry for himself. He handed over his soggy shirt and slid onto a barstool.

Emma slipped into the laundry area and deposited the shirt in the dryer. She took a moment to frown up at the ceiling. *God, is this You? Why did you bring this man here? What am I supposed to do with him?*

She didn't hang around expecting an answer, by now she knew better than that. Thomas sat staring at a spot on the floor as if his life depended on it.

"Thomas? How did you get wet? Do you want to tell me about that?"

"You look familiar. Do I know you?"

"We just met in the woods. I'm the pebble planter."

"Oh yes. Miss hopeful who wants to grow a mountain."

Emma waved over herself with a flippant hand. "One and the same. Can I make you some coffee?"

"Sure. Do I know you from somewhere else? You really are familiar."

Ordering your wedding cards, speed dating, and meeting in the woods. For two people who'd never officially met, they were building up quite a history, but it wouldn't do to have him joining all the dots just yet. Also, she intended to make good use of this time. She had him here in her house, there was no time to waste.

"I've got a very common face. People tell me that all the time."

"You're quite beautiful, actually." Thomas smiled at her, but it was a half-hearted attempt that never quite made it to his eyes.

"That's kind of you. Here's your coffee. Now tell me, did you get rained on, or did you fall in a duck pond?"

Thomas ran his fingers through his soggy hair. "My big brother is a psycho. He tipped water on me in my bed while I was sleeping."

"What?! Why would he do such a thing?" Benedict was not just a meddler, but a troublemaker too.

"I don't know the reasons behind half the things my brother does."

Emma thought about what she knew of Benedict. This was a completely accurate assessment, but she couldn't let on that she knew the man. "What would make him tip a bucket over you in bed?"

Thomas suddenly tilted his head and frowned at her. "What are you doing in this house, by the way?"

"I was hired to redo this house. Fix it up. One of the conditions was that I move onsite while the renovations are happening."

"Renovations. I see."

"Why does it matter to you? You have a connection to this house?" She laughed, "You must have, otherwise why would you have been sitting on the porch?"

Thomas glanced around with a look on his face Emma couldn't put a name to. In a moment, the lights came on. "Did you live in this house?"

"I'm impressed. This was our family home, yes."

"And my boss must be your brother."

"Benedict Holmes is your boss. You have my sympathy."

A message came through on Emma's phone and saved her from answering.

Benedict: It's too late for supper, but can I fetch you for coffee? I know a quaint place.

Just as the conversation was heading where she wanted it to. Drat. She typed a quick *yes* and waved her phone at Thomas. "My boss is on his way over for a business meeting, so it might be better if you left. As in right now. Drink that last swallow and then you have to go."

"You don't want him to know that I know you?"

"There's no time. You've got to get out of here. I don't think he'd take kindly to me having people over." *Especially not his brother who I'm not supposed to be making contact with.*

"I'm right there with you, man. The less he knows about my life, the less he can meddle."

Emma scuttled him to the door and nearly sent him out wrapped in a towel. "Your shirt!"

She'd just managed to swap out a warm, dry shirt for a soggy towel and shoo Thomas out the house when Benedict's headlights turned into the drive.

What was she doing getting involved with this family and their issues?

• • • ● • ● • • •

Benedict pulled up to the house and felt the familiar twist to his insides. Emma came out, locked the door, and trotted down the stairs wearing a pale blue sweater that looked soft and comfortable.

She got in the car took one look at him and asked, "What's wrong?"

He cursed the fact that his feelings had slipped onto his face and brushed her off. "Why should there be something wrong?"

"You just don't seem your normal joyful self."

Now she was having a dig at him, without a doubt. "What about you, you're looking flustered. What's going on with you?" The question was pure redirection. She didn't look flustered, just fully alive and glowing. He forced himself to focus on the road.

"Nothing." Her answer was too quick, too matter-of-fact. "It's ten at night. Why are we still going for coffee? Also, you look terrible. Are you sick?"

Her words bounced off him like peanuts off a sleeping elephant. He didn't want to talk. The mess of weird emotions inside seemed to be stirred up around her. Feelings. Hmm. He liked folding them away into a box in his mind and ignoring them. He had a mental cellar where that kind of thing belonged. Anything he packed away down there was untouchable. It was one of his best abilities, it allowed him to do what he needed to.

"Benedict? Are you okay?" There was a genuine note of concern to her voice that caught him.

He cleared his throat. "We're here. Come on."

They made their way up a narrow flight of stairs to a small coffee shop tucked away above an enormous bookshop that had fast become his favorite thinking place. Tonight though, he didn't want his thoughts for company, so he'd brought Emma. Not his wisest move. The girl had a way of tilting everything that was stable inside of him.

Too late.

They settled into a booth in a quiet corner and placed their orders with a waitress who was just the right level of friendly without being buddy-buddy.

Emma sat opposite him with a tiny smile playing in the corners of her mouth. He'd give anything to know what she was thinking.

Emma tucked her hair behind her ears and drew her legs up onto her chair, crossing them at the ankles. Her cheeks were pink and her skin glowed as if she'd just been for a run. She was quite breathtaking. Not his type, of course, but beautiful nonetheless.

She leaned on the table and frowned at him. "Are you sure you're okay? At the risk of getting my head bitten off, you look exhausted. Is there something bugging you?"

He stared at her for a moment. So much had happened in the last 24 hours and all of it was laced through with too little sleep. Settling a family in safety always put him on a high, but the comedown from that was wicked. It hit him harder each time. The fear of whether he'd done enough to keep them safe ate away at him like cancer.

Then there was the whole business of falling out with Thomas. Not knowing if the big lump was somewhere safe or not bothered him more than he cared to admit. If something happened to the twit while he was out on his own mission, it would be his own fault. At least, that's what Benedict told himself but he knew the guilt would be his.

Emma stirred sugar into her coffee and slid the sugar bowl to where he could reach. "What's the deal with you and your brother?"

"What makes you ask?" He slid the sugar bowl back to her without taking any.

Her eyes slid to his cup and he didn't miss the quick shake of her head or the way her eyes rolled. "You have issues with him. Why?"

"If wanting the best for someone is an issue, then yes, I do." It may have been fatigue clouding his judgment, but Emma did look awfully pretty.

"Are you listening to me?" She patted his hand and his skin tingled at her touch.

"Finish your coffee, I want to show you something." He took a moment to study the softness of her. It was so *other*. A deeply enthralling thing that made him feel at once out of his depth and completely at home.

"I'm not sure you should be going anywhere but to bed. The rings under your eyes are big enough to throw boxing matches in." She had a look in her eye he'd never seen before. He couldn't place it, but it fascinated him.

"You don't want to fight me," he said.

"I'm not a fighter."

"I think you're wrong, Emma Redwood. I think there is plenty of fight in you. You just pick your battles."

"Doesn't everybody?" She drained her last mouthful of coffee and placed the cup in the saucer, shifting it until the handle sat directly parallel to the edge of the table. "What do you want to show me?"

He pulled out her chair and helped her to her feet. "Come."

• • • • ● • ● • • • •

Emma's thoughts darted like skittish goldfish as they walked from the building across the way to a high-rise hotel close enough for their hands to brush. Something had shifted between them and she didn't know what to make of it.

Benedict greeted the sleepy security guard, who tipped his hat and waved them inside.

"Does he know you? Are we allowed in here?"

Benedict's mouth toyed with the idea of smiling. "C'mon."

The elevator seemed unimpressed at being woken up and jerked and hissed as it took them upwards. It stopped with a shudder that made Emma stumble.

Benedict waved her out first before following. "This way."

"What are we here for?" Emma blinked at the darkness on the rooftop. The moon was nowhere to be seen and this building didn't seem to have rooftop lights.

Benedict leaned in close and whispered in her ear, "Shh!"

Annoyance and intrigue tussled over her emotions and yet she felt no fear. She stopped to examine the thought, but Benedict's hand closed over hers and drew her out into the darkness.

The lack of light heightened every sensation triggered by his palm pressed warm against hers, the pressure of his fingers on the back of her hand, and how the combination of those two things made her feel more than a little light-headed.

Or maybe being on a rooftop fed her fear of heights. That was it! He was taking her right to the edge after all. Wait—

"I don't know if we should—"

He turned back towards her, *shh'd* her again whispered, "Trust me, it's worth it. Close your eyes."

She shut her eyes and let him lead her. He led her forward and let go of her hand. Cold metal sent a chill through her arms and her hands shot out to steady herself. He'd led her to a barricade of sorts.

"You can look now." His voice was a little distance off, not right in her ear as it had been.

She took a deep breath, already planning what words to throw at him for all the drama, and opened her eyes. A broad yellow moon rose slowly over the brooding darkness of the sea, sending sparkles rippling across the surface.

The height of the rooftop gave the perfect vantage point over the lights of the city to the vista beyond and her eyes drank it in. All the words she'd lined up to throw at him dissolved off her tongue and all she could do was stare.

She snuck a glance at him, only to find him staring at her instead of the view. Her heart beat furiously, she could feel the pulse in her neck. He truly was a very good-looking man. Especially by moonlight.

Heat flooded her cheeks as she looked down.

She looked *down*.

And saw the drop.

Heights were not her thing and this building was high. Her head spun and the stars seemed to shoot down from the sky to dance in her eyes.

Her vision swam and two things came into clear focus; losing strength in her knees and Benedict's strong arms like iron bands around her as blackness descended.

Chapter Sixteen

BENEDICT FELT LOGIC DISSOLVE as his eyes caught Emma's and held. The moonlight on the sea didn't move him. Neither was it merely the beauty of the woman in front of him. He'd been around many beautiful women, but none of them affected him in this way.

Everything he knew about her came crashing together in that moment. Her spunk, her passion, the way she saw life, it all came flooding into him as she stared at him so frankly with unguarded eyes.

Just as quickly, he saw her eyes drop, the shudder pass through her body and her hands go limp on the railing. He caught her as she fell. He wasn't quite ready and the sudden weight of her slamming into him nearly toppled him.

He threw his arms around her, caught his footing, braced himself, and only just managed to stay upright. Once he had her and felt confident that neither of them would be connecting the floor, he hoisted her up in his arms and carried her across to a recliner where he dumped her rather unceremoniously, swinging her second leg up next to the first.

He knelt next to her, not sure what to do next. The only thing he'd seen in movies in involved cheek-slapping and peeping under eyelids, though he had no desire to do either.

Before he could resort to movie tactics, her eyes fluttered and opened wide, filled with panic.

"You're okay. I caught you. You didn't hit your head or anything."

"I felt like I was falling." Emma sounded deeply horrified at the thought.

He bit back a laugh. "You did, but I caught you."

"I fell off the building?"

"What? No. You just flaked out. I'm assuming you have a crippling fear of heights?"

She shrugged as if mulling over the meaning of what he'd just said. "I guess so."

A wave of weariness crashed in on him. "Come on, let's go. It's late. Can you stand?"

"What kind of dumb question is that?" She pushed herself upright, wobbled, and grabbed his arm for support. She shot him a sheepish grin. "Maybe not that dumb after all."

• • • ● • ● • • •

Emma still felt a little strange in the head as the elevator doors swooshed shut behind them. Benedict seemed to take up more than his fair share of space and it wasn't helping her swimming head. The sooner he dropped her home, the better.

He was leaning against the railing watching the numbers count down and whistling softly. It all felt rather awkward.

Halfway between floor eleven and twelve, the elevator stopped. The internal lights flickered twice as if saying *au revoir* then sputtered out too.

A small sound escaped Emma's lips that came out like, "Oh."

Benedict muttered under his breath, Emma couldn't quite catch what he said, but from the tone, she wasn't sure she wanted to.

His cell light came on, a bright beam that sliced through the darkness and blinded Emma.

"Point that thing somewhere else, please."

"Oh, sorry." He aimed the light at the panel of buttons, found the emergency button, and pressed it. They couldn't hear anything so he pressed it again.

After a couple of quick presses, he gave up. "Let me phone someone." He opened up the dialer on his phone, but he couldn't get a dialing tone. "Well, that's just great."

Emma had never seen this man so out of sorts. "The guy on security who let us in, won't he come looking when we don't come out?"

Benedict rubbed his hands across his eyes. "Er, no. He went off duty shortly after he let us in. Let's get the new guy's attention." He put his phone on the floor with the light shining upwards. With that, he started banging on the door as if his life depended on it.

Emma watched him, fascinated at the intensity of the man. It might have been the lighting but noticed the man still had dark circles under his eyes that would rival a raccoon.

He stopped long enough to frown at her. "Come on. This is a team effort."

"Trust me, you're making enough noise for both of us."

Benedict said nothing but the look he gave her left no doubt that she was fully expected to participate in door banging.

"Fine. Move over." She took up her spot next to him and felt the heat from his arm next to hers.

"That's better. On the count of three." He held up one finger, then a second. His eyes locked on hers and a sneaky smile lingered in the corners of his mouth. His third finger shot up and his head flicked toward the lift door.

They started banging at the same time, but Emma found herself wanting to giggle.

He stuck his hands on his hips as he stared her down. "I get the feeling you're not taking this seriously."

She couldn't tell if he was joking or not. She forced a contrite seriousness into her expression and cleared her throat. "I'm ready now."

"You're going to smack it as hard as me?"

"I'm going to smack it ... as hard as I can."

"Go. I want to check on you."

"Benedict, I'm not smacking this door by myself. Are you quite mad?"

He grinned at her as if she'd passed some test. "Good. You know your limits. I like that." He smacked the door with the flat of his hand. "You know what, if they didn't hear that, they're not going to."

"You can try climbing out the roof panel. That always seems to work." Emma tried to keep her face deadpan. Why she had the urge to laugh when he was so serious, was beyond her.

"The roof panel? Emma. My dear Emma. You're such a dreamer. Do you honestly think we're in some book?"

"Well, do you have any better ideas?" She faced him, bolder than ever before.

He leaned in close, so close their noses nearly touched. "In fact, I do." With that, he started undoing his belt and Emma backed away so fast, she bumped into the side.

"Relax, woman. I have a plan. If I can just get the edge of this buckle in between the two doors, I might be able to get my fingers in." He grunted as he got to work on the doors. "Hold the light for me?"

Emma picked up his phone and aimed it where he was working. It had noticeably dimmed from when they'd first got stuck in the lift.

"What's your battery on?" She checked the screen. "We're at twelve percent. That's not going to last—"

Thick blackness flooded in as his phone sang a little tune and switched itself off.

"I was about to say, it dies fast when it hits twelve."

The darkness was so thick, there was no way to see her hand before her face. Emma felt panic rising.

Shuffling sounds came from across the space. Benedict was putting his belt back on.

"You okay over there?"

"Sort of." She was proud of the fact that her voice only quivered once.

"Alright, come to my voice. I'm just going to keep talking until you're here."

Emma bumped into him and he took her hands in his. "How about we sit down here for a while?"

They slid down the side of the elevator together, Benedict still holding both of Emma's hands in his. The warmth of his hands calmed her as they settled in side by side.

· · · ● · ● · ● · · ·

Benedict had to keep Emma's mind off being stuck in the dark, he could feel her panic rising. She'd pulled her hands away the moment they were safely down.

"So, Emma. Tell me, what did you want to be when you were growing up?"

"What has that got to do with anything?"

"Humor me. I'll answer anything you want to ask me."

"Oh, but you can't laugh. It's a bit silly."

"No laughing. It can't be that bad."

Emma cleared her throat and he felt her tuck her hair behind her ears. "You know when you choose paint colors, they all have names? Like purple cow, or Bahama blue?"

"I hope neither of those is on your wish list for the house," Benedict answered slowly not sure where she was going with this.

"You probably wouldn't know this, but when you buy nail polish, each color is named too. The same with eyeshadow colors. Some are really whacked like Hot Sand, Second Day Bruise. Haven't you always wanted your nails done in two layers of Undercooked Beef, Vegan Green, or Lump of Clay? Hmmm?"

"I'm so glad I'm a dude right now. You've no idea. But where are you going with this? You can't change the subject. I'll just bring it straight back."

She patted his arm. "Naming colors. That's the whole point. I wanted to be the one who got to name all the colors."

"That's not even a real job."

He felt Emma's arm move in what he envisioned as a shrug. "Somebody has to do it."

"Seriously though, why would anyone want toenails painted in Lump of Clay?"

"You joke, but it's one of my favorites. Anyway, what about you? What did you want to be?"

In the dark, he couldn't tell if she was joking or serious. Either way, he'd have to be convincing to satisfy her. "There was one moment that stood out to me. I was about ten. My friend and I were swimming at the local pool and a little girl went under. Nobody noticed, except for the guy raking leaves. I watched him toss the rake, and jump into the water fully clothed, shoes and all to rescue her. By the time the lifeguard noticed something was going down, the cleaning guy already had her head above water and was swimming to the side. She was a little shaken up, but she recovered just fine. I've never wanted to be anything but that man."

"A caretaker at a public swimming pool?" She paused long enough for him to wonder if she'd missed the point of his whole touching story. "Kidding. You want to rescue people."

"Now you're on the right track."

"For fame and glory?"

"Oh no. Not at all. Nobody, other than me even noticed what went down. He just did it because it was the right thing to do."

"So ... do you feel like what you did with Thomas was rescuing him?" There was an edge to her voice that screamed *thin ice.*

"Let me tell you something. Thomas doesn't love Daniella as much as he thinks he does. It's easy to see from the outside, but harder for him because he's blinded by what he thinks is love. I did the boy a favor."

"I don't know. I think you're wrong."

"And I don't want to talk about it." He injected a lighter tone into his words, hoping it would fix where this was going.

"Me neither." Emma laughed. "Did we just agree on something? That's quite a momentous occasion."

"We should celebrate." Benedict bit back a laugh.

"I agree with that too. Two in a row. It's a new record."

Agree. Let play this or that. I'll start." His mind flipped through all the random trivia he had stored up for occasions like this. Not that he'd ever thought he'd need to be prepared to be stuck in a lift in the dark with a beautiful lady for this long before.

"Beach or city?"

Emma didn't hesitate. "Oh, that's easy. Beach." She moved around next to him. "This floor is getting cold now. Your turn, what's your idea of the perfect date?"

"Hmm. I don't know if that question should be allowed. You've already told me that I'm not the dating type." He listened to her breathing next to him. She'd calmed right down. Regardless of what they'd spoken of. Mission accomplished.

"Humor me. Maybe I judged you too quickly."

"You're forgiven. A date? It's been a while. Probably just the usual, candles, dinner, good conversation. I'm a simple guy."

"No, I'm not buying it." If there were lights on, she'd be glaring at him right now.

"Fine. Hiking in the Himalayas or exploring a coral reef off an exotic island coastline somewhere. Although I must say, getting stuck in a lift is pretty nice too. Is that better?"

"That's more like it. Except for the lift part."

"I'll have to make a note of that for the future." He spoke quickly before she could comment. "My turn. What are your thoughts on God?"

Emma didn't hesitate. "I couldn't live without Him. You?"

Heat shot through him at her answer. He took a moment to compose his thoughts, then cleared his throat before speaking. "I'm not religious, but I know He hears me when I talk to Him and I do my best to listen when He speaks. He is the only reason life makes sense."

"I agree." Emma's simple words settled between them as a broad field of common ground that reframed everything he thought he knew about her.

Their conversation wound on, dipping into seriousness, only to float up high to silliness and slip back easily to halfway between the two as hours slid by unnoticed.

• • • • ● • ● ● • •

Benedict was leaning back against the side of the elevator when Emma heard his breathing change. He was falling asleep. Slowly, infinitely slowly, he tipped sideways until his forehead rested on her shoulder.

Within five minutes, her neck was going into spasm and she knew she had to move him. She prodded his arm to wake him up but that did nothing. With some careful wriggling, she got him to slide off her shoulder and she maneuvered herself so that his head landed neatly in her lap. She eased out her neck and heard the clicks in her spine.

Benedict sighed contentedly and slipped his arm under her legs to hug her calves. Emma sat frozen, completely out of her depth for dealing with this.

There was no doubt in her mind, the man was tired. She'd seen it in his face over coffee. Even the way he'd lost the sharp edge of professionalism he always hid behind.

Deep exhaustion was only the only explanation for that.

The kindest thing she could do here, trapped in the dark, was to let the man sleep. Her arms had been hovering, she didn't know where to put them. She couldn't keep that up all night.

Surrendering to the moment she rested one on his arm and held his head with the other. Any other position would have made her cramp up within minutes.

His breathing deepened and slowed and she felt her heart rate settle in time to each breath he drew. When he moved, she felt the tension in his arm muscles, and as he settled again, the relaxation flowed in as a deep heaviness.

Emma sat in the dark trying to figure out the mystery of the man who was currently using her legs as a pillow. Everything she'd seen and heard of him was at odds with the vulnerable side she'd seen tonight. Or was it?

Thomas and Dani both had strong opinions, though likely clouded by their broken hearts. There was no way to figure out the heart of this man using logic or the opinions of other people. Only God knew what was going on inside him anyway, why didn't she start there in the first place? Emma shut her eyes, leaned her head back against the elevator wall, and had a deep conversation with Jesus about Benedict Holmes.

Chapter Seventeen

BENEDICT GRIMACED EACH TIME a memory of the night before popped up in his head. He needed to manage himself better. Exhaustion messed with him. It was simply *not good*.

They'd been rescued at about half-past-four in the morning. Between their deep chats and being rescued was a long period of time that he had no memory of. Apparently, he'd slept on Emma's legs for hours. *Hours.*

It would be easier if he never had to face her again, but that wasn't going to happen. There was no point avoiding it. The longer he stayed away, the more awkward it would all be.

He couldn't shake the lingering effects of being close to her. All he had to do was close his eyes and he could feel her warmth, the scent of her skin...

Stop it!

It was time to face her in broad daylight and put everything back into order. They had a meeting with the kitchen planner at 9 a.m. That gave him just enough time to shower, shave, and drive across to the house.

• • • • ● • ● • • •

Emma never slept in, but after the night spent in a lift, she was in no hurry to get moving. She lay on her side, watching the play of light through the leaves that made dancing shadows on the curtain, and wondered what to do with herself.

Last night was a completely knotted-up ball of emotions that she daren't unpick for fear that it would unravel her at the same time.

The side of Benedict that she'd seen was so unexpected, it had caught her off guard. She would never have imagined being so comfortable with him in the dark, in such a small place for so many hours.

And yet...

A car pulled up outside. She mentally ran through a list of deliveries and meetings that were scheduled but she knew there was nothing for today. She shot out of bed and peeped through a gap in the curtain.

Benedict had pulled up outside and was letting himself in. Her mind flew through reasons why he might be here but she came up with a single reason and the thought of it made her tummy flip.

She threw on clothes, checked herself in the mirror, *yikes*, and headed downstairs.

Benedict was in the kitchen, leaning on the countertop going through her file. She kept a file of her ideas and inspiration for the house. It was more for her own use, yet here he was, paging through it.

"Did I miss something? You're here early."

He straightened up at the sound of her coming in but took his time turning around. When he did, her jaw clenched. The hard edges were back.

It was as if last night had never happened.

"I booked this meeting with you a week ago. The kitchen consultant will be here in..." he checked his watch, "five minutes."

Emma's mind flew, trying to recall if she'd received the notification as she always did. She drew a blank.

"I don't remember that booking, I'm sorry. Do you want some coffee to wake up? I don't think either of us got enough proper sleep."

He didn't even glance at her. "No, that won't be necessary. Have you chosen tiles?"

Emma stood dumbstruck. What game was this man playing? "My suggestions are all there. You just need to come up with alternatives or approve them."

His eyes didn't leave the file as he paged through the 'kitchen' section. "Oh, here. Serene Sandstone. So you're leaning warmer rather than cooler?"

"For this kitchen, yes." A million justifications lined up at her lips. A million reasons. Waiting to spew out and convince him she was right. She bit down hard and held her ground.

"Let's see what the expert says."

On cue, the doorbell rang.

Emma felt sick at the change in Benedict. The doorbell was a useful excuse to flee. The consultant she let in was a small man dressed in slim-fitting black. He tilted his head in greeting. His hair stood straight up—a short, blue-black, buzz cut.

He breezed straight past her and through to the kitchen as if he'd been in the house a hundred times before. Emma followed him, thinking that this day and all its weirdness were just too much for the amount of sleep she'd had.

Benedict introduced her as she walked in. "Kevin, this is Emma. She's overseeing the renovations."

Kevin tipped his head again and it made Emma wonder how old he was. He didn't look old, but she could see by the sunlight streaming through the kitchen windows that he wasn't young either. There were years of life lurking behind the polite smile.

"Hi, Kevin. I've put together some ideas, but obviously, Mr. Holmes has the final say."

Kevin, who seemed monk-like in his commitment to silence, slid a laptop onto the counter and opened it.

He moved aside and motioned for the two of them to take their seats. Emma sat down next to Benedict with a lump in her throat that was either pain or rage.

Suddenly monk-Kevin found his voice. It was a deep, melodious sound that made Emma want to stare at him. That voice from such a small person?

"As you can see, I've taken the liberty of uploading images of your kitchen. All our stock is on the system. No more guessing what's going on." He ended his delivery with a tight smile that might as well have been cut and pasted from a sales textbook.

Emma deliberately avoided looking at Benedict. "Not having to guess what's going on will be such a relief. Thank you." She kept her eyes glued on the laptop screen, yet she *felt* the look Benedict shot her way.

"Nothing to guess about here. It's all pretty straightforward the way I see it." He shrugged and selected the combination that Emma suggested. "What do you think, Kev?"

Kevin slid in behind them and muttered under his breath, tilting his head this way and that. "It's a little pedestrian."

Emma bristled. "Well, excuse me. If you two want to make your decisions, I'm going to carry on in the other room. Let me know when you're done. I'll catch up with you on the other side."

Benedict's eyes were dark and unreadable. "Emma, don't be like that. I employed you for this exact reason. Your way of seeing things is different from how we do. Defend your choices."

She stared at him with a hundred words tumbling through her mind. She bit hard to keep them there.

"You want my opinion? Here goes. This kitchen," she waved her hand across the room, and she could have sworn his way too, "as it is now is very closed off and cold." She stared him straight in the eye, and he knew she wasn't just talking about the kitchen.

"Oh is that so?"

"More than that, the light fixture, which I'm sure used to be quite normal, gives off light that is harsh and unfriendly."

Benedict glared at her and she felt her hands slide to her hips, challenging him to cross her.

"Well, Miss Redwood, I'll have you know that this light fitting does what it needs to, to get things done."

"I'm sorry, but I think you're completely wrong. You seem to forget the purpose of light fittings."

"Oh, and what may that be?" Benedict's voice had dropped dangerously low. Emma recognised it by now, but she couldn't stop herself. She didn't want to.

"That's another thing. The space in here is suffocating, staid, and stuck up. I don't know if anything I do could fix that. Frankly, a kitchen has to *want* to change and I don't think this one does." Her arms slid across her chest.

Kevin breathed extra loudly. "Are you two done?"

Emma, still glaring at Benedict answered, "Oh I'm done. So done."

Benedict's eyes held hers for a few seconds before he turned away to face Kevin. "Why don't you show us what you've got?"

Kevin blinked once and carried on as if nothing strange was going on. "Emma, what you've put together here—"

"Yes, I know. It's *pedestrian*."

A faint smile touched Kevin's lips. He was a strangely gentle creature, even though he'd ignored her when he first came in. He waved her closer.

"You'll see what I mean when I explain it."

She sat down dutifully with a heavy sigh.

"Your color combination is perfect for the amount of light that comes in as the room is now. Here's where I'd like to make a suggestion." He tapped the screen with his pen. "I'd suggest we break this wall down and create an open plan flow between the kitchen and dining room. We install cupboards that hang from the ceiling here," another tap on the screen, "and light them inside. Like this." With a few clicks, he'd made the changes. The result was gorgeous.

"I like that. I didn't realize we could break down walls."

Kevin looked over to Benedict who nodded once. "We can break down walls."

Emma stared at the results of their combined efforts. This kitchen was going to be gorgeous by the time it was done. "This is good. I'm happy."

Benedict added another single nod.

Kevin glanced at them both and started packing up his bits and pieces. "Great. I'll organize the team and we'll see you bright and early tomorrow."

Benedict walked the man out and Emma's shock at the difference in the man between last night and this morning came flooding back. She braced herself. The moment he stepped back into the room, she was going to tackle him again.

He came in reading a message on his phone. He slid it into his pocket. "That's settled then. The team will be in tomorrow. I'd suggest you set up a basic kitchen in another room while they work."

"So we're going to pretend last night just didn't happen?"

"Do you need help setting up a temporary place to cook?"

Emma regarded him with cool eyes. "You *drooled* on my legs, Benedict."

"I'm assuming that's a no?" Benedict lifted an eyebrow in question.

Emma felt her blood boil. "I see how it is. Fine."

"That's a no, then."

• • • ● • ● ● • • •

Emma watched Benedict's car leave. She was so frustrated she almost looked for something to throw at him as he left. Almost.

It would seem that Benedict the boss-man was firmly back in place and last night was to be swept under the carpet or locked away like whatever was hidden in the cellar.

Instead, she went back inside and started moving furniture. The dining room table was solid oak and heavier than an ox. She pulled and pushed, sweated, and used muscles she'd forgotten existed but the table didn't budge.

"Can I help?"

Emma spun around looking for a weapon to defend herself. "Thomas! You scared me half to death!" Thomas was back, still wearing the same clothes he'd been in two days ago. He was unshaven and didn't smell great. Emma had to stop herself from holding her nose.

"I knocked but you didn't hear. The door was open, so..." His hands flew in an elegant visual ta-da. "Are you all good? You look a bit unhappy."

"Your brother just left." She stopped to rein in her words. "He is a frustrating man. Let's just leave it at that."

Thomas barked a dry laugh. "Big surprise. So basically he tossed an emotional bucket of cold water over you. Yes?"

"That is one hundred percent accurate."

"That's what he does. Come on, let me help you move this thing. Where'd you want it?"

Emma frowned. "I need to set up a temporary kitchen in here, so this must move closer to the window."

Without much explaining from Emma, Thomas caught the idea of what she needed and within half an hour, she had a fully operational mini-kitchen set up in the dining room. She went through to the kitchen to make Thomas a cup of thank you tea and found a notebook she didn't recognize sitting on the countertop.

She picked it up to investigate, flipped it open, and found an exquisitely sketched Dani staring back at her.

Thomas swooped in and pulled it out of her hands. "That's mine."

"Did you draw that?"

"It makes me feel better. To draw her. It eases the ache for a little while." He shook his head and slipped the book into his jacket pocket.

Emma fought with herself. Boldness won. "This is a bit weird, but humor me. I'd like to see it. If that's okay with you?"

Thomas stared at her, sighed, then dug in his pocket and slid the book across the countertop.

Emma slid onto a kitchen stool and opened it up. The first page was covered in vines and leaves. If it were wallpaper, she'd use it in the dining room. "Your shading is good. Very good."

She turned the page and found Dani. She wore a long dress that blew in the wind and stared down at a dandelion in her hands. Her long hair rode the wind too, the twisting and twirling caught perfectly in a moment in pencil.

Emma shot a glance at Thomas. The poor boy was so far gone, he wasn't even watching her to see her reaction. He was zoned out in his own world.

The next page was her hand holding a rope. "Is she on a swing in this one?"

Thomas came back from far away and nodded. "How did you know?"

"Something in the angle of her hand maybe? Though honestly, it's just because you are so good." She started turning pages faster. The moon peeping out from behind the clouds. A chubby laughing baby. A dewdrop off the tip of a leaf with sunlight sparkling through it. All punctuated with sketches of Dani.

She closed the book and held on to it. "You're still in love with her, aren't you?"

Thomas leaned on his elbows, spine bent like a fern over the cup of coffee she'd slid in front of him. "Even if I am, it doesn't matter. I don't add anything good to her life. I would be so bad for her."

"Did Benedict tell you that?"

His eyes flashed up to meet hers briefly. "He didn't have to. I know it."

Emma let that one slide for the moment. "What are you going to do with this talent?"

Thomas started as if she'd just woken him up. "Excuse me? What do you mean?"

"You have serious talent. What are you going to do with it?"

"Drawing isn't a real thing. It's not a proper job."

"Oh don't tell me. Benedict told you that."

Thomas shook his head. "Oh no, I wouldn't even mention this to him."

"Next question. If you could do this as your job. Would you?"

"Draw? For a living? That wouldn't work."

"Just play along. Imagine being able to draw and get paid for it. Would that work for you?"

Thomas shrugged. "Obviously. I'm happy when I'm drawing. Well, *happier*."

Emma drummed her fingers on the cover. "Do you mind if I hang onto this for a few days? I have someone I'd like to show it to. With your permission of course."

"Be my guest. I have tons of drawings. I can't see what good it's going to do."

"Great! I don't know if anything will come of it, but it's worth a shot."

Thomas sat all slumped on the chair, looking like he hadn't slept in days.

"Thomas?"

"Hmm?"

"Do me a favor. Go home."

He started to object, but she flung up a hand with such force, he swallowed his words and blinked, going a bit squint.

"Right now. Go home, talk to your brother, take a nice long shower, shave, for goodness sake, use some deodorant. Leave this with me. I get the feeling your life is about to change for the better." She watched him sway in his seat from exhaustion. Wherever he'd been for the last few days, he hadn't slept much.

She reached across and squeezed his limp hand. "Do you trust me?"

His eyes slid up slowly to meet hers. Then she got the one thing she was hoping for. A single nod.

"Good. Change of plan, I'm taking you home. Come with me."

Chapter Eighteen

Benedict sat at his desk in the study, thinking things through. He'd hoped Thomas would be home when he arrived back, but he wasn't. This was getting ridiculous. He didn't think anything was seriously wrong with the boy. His insides would be giving him no peace if that were the case.

Letting his guard down around Emma the night before was proving to be a problem. He was going to have to be doubly distant now to recover from his lapse. He put her out of his mind and opened up the text he'd received back at the house.

COR HQ: House needed for two. Extraction planned for a week from now. More details to follow.

He reached under the desk and pressed a hidden switch. A secret drawer popped out and he removed his laptop and set it up. It sat flashing, waiting for fingerprint access.

The screen opened up to a list of locations and he turned he prayed as he scanned through them all. "Where should we put these two, Jesus?"

"Put which two?" Thomas stood leaning on the doorframe, looking haggard.

"You're back." He shut his laptop with more force than he intended. "You look terrible."

Thomas shrugged. "At least I've dried off now."

"I regret nothing."

"Of course, you don't." Thomas's face had a hard edge to it that Benedict had never seen before.

"You still don't get it, do you?"

Thomas pushed himself off the door frame. It was a slow, calculated move. "And you've never got me."

"So what's your plan? Are you going to live off your trust fund money forever?" Benedict held back, the question came out less harsh than it could have.

"I'm waiting for the right opportunity to present itself. Then I'll figure it out." He eyed his big brother sideways. "Though I'm sure that doesn't fit into your tidy plans."

Benedict leaned back in his chair with his elbows propped up on the armrests, fingers tented across his chest. "Where did you go?" He bit back Daniella's name. That would send the boy over the edge.

Thomas shrugged. "Here and there."

A message came through on Benedict's phone. It was time to go. "Listen, I've got to go. What are you going to do while I'm gone?"

"What's it to you?"

"Make sure you eat. Do something. Take a shower." Thomas watched him leave, leaning on the front door frame.

Benedict felt the stab inside, something wasn't right. For the first time in a long time, he felt torn between his job and his family. It unsettled him.

• • • ● • ● • • •

Emma braced herself for facing Brenda. As much as she was uncomfortable around the woman, Brenda was the one they needed right now.

She pep-talked herself all the way upstairs to Brenda's apartment. She'd hoped they could meet at the studio, but Brenda had arranged to meet her here instead. It was so much more intimidating. *Take one for the team, Em. Life is not all about you. This guy needs a break.*

She was about to tell herself to shut it when the door opened to Brenda in all her green-clad glory.

"Emma. Come inside dear girl. Are you coming to update me on a certain Mr. Holmes?"

Emma forced a grin onto her face. *Take. One. For. The. Team. Ugh* ... "No, in fact, I'm here to find out a bit more about the art gallery that you run. You get to choose what goes in there, right?"

"That's generally how it works." Brenda was looking at her as if she was a fruitcake. "Have you got some work to show me? This isn't exactly the place for rock art."

Emma hauled the notebook out of her bag and handed it over. "A friend of mine, not me."

"Let's go sit on the patio. The sun is nice at this time of the day."

Emma's heart was in her throat as they sat down in two canvas chairs. Brenda took her time, fussing over the angle of her chair, before turning around and carefully lowering herself down. She wasn't a small woman, and her body seemed to be giving her trouble.

The notebook looked small in her hands and Emma berated herself for even thinking this was a good idea. She was just glad she hadn't brought Thomas along in person. Poor guy was struggling enough without being on the receiving end of Brenda's feistiness.

Brenda clicked her fingers as if she was about to play a piano piece, then slowly started paging. Her face gave nothing away and it left Emma wondering if she'd done a silly thing.

After a long time paging, Brenda closed the final cover and sat with the book between her palms. "Who is this guy?"

Emma knew she shouldn't namedrop. Not right now. Brenda was already obsessed with Benedict. She would lap up the chance to get on the in with his brother.

"His name is Thomas. So what do you think?"

"I won't beat around the bush. I've just received a commission to decorate a new game lodge. I feel like this style would work perfectly in the restaurant. Can he draw wildlife?"

"Give me a mo." Emma pulled out her phone and typed in a quick message and hit send. "Let's see what he says."

Within a few seconds, her phone beeped. "Wildlife is completely doable."

Brenda nearly smiled but managed to hang on to her sour face. "Have him meet me tomorrow at nine, at the studio." She flipped through the notebook thoughtfully one last time. "This is all so lucky."

Emma couldn't stop grinning. "I think it's more like a clever plan made in Heaven, but that's just my personal opinion."

• • • ● • ● • • •

Benedict liked his extraction ops to run like clockwork, smooth and accurate. This one was messy and nearly ended in disaster. A gust of wind banged the little guy's finger in the car door as he was climbing in the vehicle. Who knew such a tiny kid could have such a big voice?

The bedroom light came on as they drove off and the mom nearly had a panic attack. Benedict found a lollipop in his stash of secret weapons and handed it over which sorted out one of the two issues. With his attention split between calming the mom and navigating dark roads, he saw the rock in the middle of the road just in time to swerve and avoid it.

That seemed to sober the mom. She got her breathing under control, squeezed her little boy too tight, and sat shaking violently, but no longer spiraling.

He'd delivered them safely to their new home and started the long drive home just as the sun broke the horizon. Getting families to safety no longer moved him emotionally, instead, it satisfied a deep restlessness inside.

It never lasted long, but for a little while, he had peace.

This time, the restlessness didn't leave. It churned inside, worse than before as if he swallowed hot chili peppers.

It all came back to Thomas. Benedict was filled with unspoken fears for his little brother, things he didn't want to think about. As he drove, he prayed. Asking for help not to get angry. Anger always lowered his capacity. It blinded him.

Chapter Nineteen

EMMA TRIPPED OVER A pile of dirty laundry and caught herself on the wall just before her face collided with it. Living in a house while renovating wasn't for the faint-hearted. It was time to create some order.

Benedict had kept himself scarce since the lift episode and the awkward morning after. Emma hated it when things were unresolved, but it was up to Benedict to fix things and she had a feeling he had no intention of doing so.

She'd been starting to feel quite fond of this echo-ey house, but now she wanted it restored and finished so she could cut ties and move on.

Emma rounded up the laundry she'd just tripped over and dumped it in the bin at the door. Her bed was already made, but she pulled the cover straight again out of habit.

She packed the pile of clean clothes into the cupboard and her hand connected with the container that had Thomas and Dani's invitations in progress. It might be time to face the fact that it was a lost cause. Those two had such issues to work through but they weren't ready to face them or talk to each other. There's not much one can do in a situation like that.

She took her carefully packed box to the kitchen. She didn't have the heart to dump it in the garbage bin, but she put it on the floor next to the garbage bin. Close enough.

The sting of defeat was swift and bitter.

It didn't take long to tame her environment. It was such a simple, silly thing – how much power a clean room had over the state of her insides.

Time to flatten the next thing that was bothering her – the terrarium. She'd found a set of keys hanging inside a cupboard in the master bedroom, one an ornate old-style key that fitted perfectly into the terrarium lock.

Emma twisted the key in the lock, pried at the door, and felt a flood of satisfaction as it door swung wide open.

The room itself was slightly bigger than the living room and would have been beautiful. Now, it was an overgrown mess, weeds had taken over and choked all the plants but there was still life in the place. A natural stream ran through the middle of it, a mere trickle of water.

A thrill shot through her. Restoring this was going to be her biggest challenge yet. Maybe ... She toyed with the idea, rolling it around in her mind and weighing it up. She'd been leaving snacks for Invisible James and he was spending a lot of energy guarding her even though she didn't need it.

Maybe she could rope him in to bring life back to this space? She'd leave a request and instructions with the batch of scones she intended leaving for lunch.

With that decided, she took her Bible and settled onto an old swing right in the middle of the overgrown tangle of plants. It was time to find out what Heaven had to say about this house, Thomas and Dani, and Benedict, too.

• • • • ● • ● ● • • •

Benedict woke with a jolt as if his brother had decided to repay the bucket of cold water. With his heart pounding, he felt the duvet.

It was dry and warm. Shards of memories flooded back and the image that had woken him popped up in his mind.

He'd been dreaming. A long, full-color saga that had moved from scene to scene, switching storylines the way a train would at a crossing, but always revolving around Emma.

The details were vague and as fleeting as mist on the wind, diaphanous and coy. If he tried to focus on them, they dissipated. The feeling of the dream, however, lingered with such force it took his breath away.

Floating bits of gold fell like snowflakes. Emma laughed and danced with her face towards the sky. Each time a flake landed on her skin, it sank into her and made her glow more. She'd turned to him, radiant, grabbed his hand, and started running.

She didn't stop when something blocked their path, she just kept running, passing straight through the obstacles as if they didn't exist.

Everything he thought would stop them, she simply ran straight through. Even as the details of the dream dissipated, he couldn't shake the feeling of intimacy that lingered.

• • • ● • ● • • •

The Bible plan she was following meant she'd be reading from Exodus, Psalms, Proverbs, and the book of James.

Not in the mood for Old Testament, she flipped to the back to find James, and her Bible fell open at a verse she'd highlighted years before.

"Now faith is the substance of things hoped for and the evidence of things not yet seen."

It slammed into her with such force she flinched.

"What are you saying, Lord?" She tried to turn the page and move on, but she just couldn't. The verse sat there on the pages of her Bible like a glowing rune in a fantasy movie.

She'd read it about twenty times when a knock on the terrarium door interrupted her. It wasn't like Benedict to knock. Maybe the man had finally learned some manners.

The door swung back and there stood Thomas with a portfolio bag under his arm.

"Hey."

"What are you doing here?"

He gestured to the bag under his arm. "You got me a commission. Thank you." He grinned at her and his eyes almost joined in. "The builders let me in, I hope you don't mind."

A jolt of happiness shot through Emma. "You're going to do it! That's great. I'm so happy it's working out. Did you just come to let me know?"

Thomas looked a little sheepish. "Well, I was wondering if you'd mind if I work here?"

"Here, in this overgrown mess?" Emma laughed at the thought.

"No, not right here, though I loved this place growing up. I thought maybe the room at the end of the house. The one that gets so much sun."

"Why, though?"

Thomas shrugged. "I feel better here. I can't work at home, not with my *big brother* issues."

"I can't argue with that. You'll have to tell him at some point. For now, make yourself at home." She paused for a moment, it was weird to think that Thomas and Benedict had grown up in this house. "Thomas, what was this area like when you lived here?"

He shrugged. "We were never allowed in. I think my mom used this as her sanctuary to get away from us when we got too much for her. As you can imagine, we weren't quiet little boys."

"And the cellar? What happened in there?"

Thomas's face twisted strangely. "That was Benedict's kingdom. I wasn't allowed in there either."

"You poor thing! Where was your space?" Emma could imagine him as a sensitive soul, always being left out.

"I didn't mind. I liked being by myself. The garden out front was my kingdom. I was always happy out there, listening to the trees whisper. It was a good way to grow up. Right, let me go get set up."

Thomas whistled an off-key tune as he turned to go. He got halfway across the bridge and stopped dead to study the trickle of water in the riverbed for a moment. "Look, there's a mini cave-in on that side. I have a feeling that's blocking up the flow."

Thomas hopped down and skittered across the rocks with sure feet like a mountain goat. He got to work on the cave-in, tossing rocks out the way and scraping through the mud with his bare hands. It didn't take long for water to start flowing and as it did, it cleared away the last of the mud. Thomas rinsed the mud off his hands and surveyed the river with deep satisfaction.

"Thomas, that's incredible!" The sound of running water filled Emma with joy. "Thank you." The joy was quickly suppressed when she thought of the implications of Thomas working here in the house.

He tipped his head in a semi-bow and made his way down the passage leaving Emma to frown at his back. Benedict wouldn't appreciate his brother working here where they were renovating.

The kitchen team was in full swing when the lounge team arrived and got to work stripping out the old fitted carpet to reveal parquet flooring underneath. Why someone would choose to cover that up with an ugly old carpet was beyond her.

She painted sample swatches on the wall and by 10 a.m. decided it was time for tea. She filled a mug and took it through to Thomas who'd set himself up in the covered patio on the far side of the house. Sunlight streamed in through the windows. He'd brought a portable easel and was completely engrossed in the work before him.

Emma caught the look on his face and the same feeling washed through her as when she read the faith verse earlier that morning. The usual insecurity was completely absent and he painted with confidence and authority. Emma tried to stop staring. The change was too much for her to comprehend.

He straightened up and stepped back to assess his work and Emma imagined him staring at Dani with that fierce confidence.

Looking at him now, she had no doubt they were right for each other. More than anything, she could see them still getting married one day. How they'd get to that point from where they were now, she had no idea. But it had to happen.

"Er, Emma?"

"What?" She'd zoned out and he'd been talking to her.
"Is that tea for me, by any chance?"
"Yes. Yes, of course." She handed it over and nearly slopped it over his hand in her rush. "I have to go do something quickly."

She ran from the room and down to the garbage she'd put out earlier that morning. She snatched up the container and clutched it to her chest. This was right and good.

Until Benedict's car pulled up in the driveway. That made her panic.

Chapter Twenty

EMMA CLIMBED THE STAIRS to rock painting feeling old. Benedict hadn't stayed long, he'd just popped in to check on the progress of things, but he'd seemed distracted and tired. Emma had been ready to fight him on any number of issues, but he'd simply refused to rise to the challenge. It was rather unsatisfying.

She'd been terrified of Benedict discovering Thomas, but one had stayed in the lounge, the other in his makeshift studio and soon after arriving, Benedict had left.

Thomas had put in a full day's painting and had left about half an hour before she was due at rock painting.

With no time to cook, she'd downed a peanut butter sarmie and a quick cup of tea. It took a few seconds to run a brush through her hair and she was ready.

Dani was happily chatting to Brenda when Emma got upstairs. Seeing Dani after her wedding revelation sent a jolt through Emma's body. She wished she had the courage to just walk up to Dani and demand to know why she and Thomas weren't together anymore.

Emma threw out a general *hello*, found a rock that vaguely inspired her, and settled in to paint it. A sultry cat took shape on her cold stone and she painted in the details vaguely wishing it was real.

She shot a glance at what Dani was doing. Flowers. Flowers seemed like a good place to start. She'd sketched them roughly, then got to work painting a bouquet in shades of pink. The background of the rock was transforming into a delicate concoction of white.

"That's pretty!" Emma said to Dani. "I love the way the pink contrasts with the gray."

"I do too." She set the bouquet aside and picked up the next rock. Emma watched as she sketched a crown. The colors seemed to choose themselves and half an hour later, she was done. The background was a soft blur that could be a veil.

Emma leaned over from the cat she was working on and frowned. Dani definitely had a wedding thing going on. "That's a tiara. I love how you've managed to make it sparkle."

"I was thinking of a crown, but you're right. It's more of a tiara than a crown."

Dani sighed and Emma looked up just in time to catch the pain in her eyes before her I'm fine mask slipped back into place.

"I love your cat."

"I'm thinking of getting one. Like an actual one."

"If you do, I'm coming with you to choose. I love cats."

"I'd probably need a more settled place to live first. I do sort of have a pet now. A spider has adopted me."

Dani's look was sheer horror. "I hate spiders."

"I used to. I'm rethinking it all now." Emma stared at this girl that she was fast becoming friends with and wondered whether the rocks were a sign of softening. Dani's first rocks had been gloomy enough to border on depressing. But these were lighter, more hopeful.

Emma just needed her to open up to her about what had gone wrong. Maybe if they hung out, the opportunity would present itself. "Do you want to come and watch a movie at my place sometime?"

Dani grinned. "Depends what we watch. I don't think I could do sappy."

"I seldom do sappy, you're safe." Emma couldn't help laughing.

• • • ● ● • ● ● • • •

Benedict frowned at Emma. They were standing in the lounge of the project house and she was being stubborn. Their current argument centered around a large wooden room divider shelf-type thing that presided over the entrance hall on one side and the living room on the other.

A week had passed since their elevator incident and things between them were slowly slipping back into their usual pre-elevator patterns. Except for the minor inconvenience of Emma being feistier than before.

"Benedict, listen to me. It is going to change the whole character of this room if we get the shelf out."

"I'm not disagreeing with you. I just don't think it will be for the better."

Emma's hands flew to her hips and her head was tilted sideways in a way that made her hair swing. She breathed sharply for a few moments and Benedict braced himself for the flood of words and emotions.

Bring it on, Emma Redwood, I'm ready.

But instead of letting fly, everything about her softened. "Would you like tea or coffee?'

"Coffee, but come back here. We need to resolve this." His voice trailed after her never quite reaching their mark.

He studied the room and tried to picture it without the bookshelf that had been there his whole life. He tilted his head, wondering if it would make a difference. It didn't.

Why was he so hung up on keeping the ugly thing? That was the actual truth, it was ugly. But he was used to it.

Emma came back with a tray and set it down on the table in the middle of the chaotic lounge. She retrieved two big pillows from underneath a dust cloth and set them down on opposite sides of the tray. Then she came and took him by the arm and led him to a cushion. Her hands were cool on his hot skin and he suppressed a shiver.

"I'm not dressed for this. You'll make me split my pants."

"Don't be such an old man. Just sit. Take your shoes off, get comfortable."

Benedict lowered himself gingerly onto the oversized cushion. He did *not* take his shoes off but kept them on in a mini-rebellion all of his own.

He was about to start up the bookshelf conversation when Emma shoved a plate his way. "There, try one of these. I baked them this morning. What do you think?"

On his plate sat a crumbly cookie of sorts, with a pinkish filling that looked like strawberry jam. Curiosity got the better of him and he took a bite. The flavors that danced on his tongue were a magnificent mix of sweet and tangy with an underlying snap that stopped it from being purely sweet.

He wanted to say how good it was but thought better of it. He imagined spray-painting Emma in cookie crumbs and settled for some wild nodding, a sigh, and a thumbs up. If these were home-baked, this girl was a keeper. For someone else, of course.

He chewed and swallowed in silence, everything else shoved aside for the moment. She sat quietly sipping her tea, her eyes on him the whole time. He pretended not to notice, but he felt them. *Keep looking, Emma.*

Once he'd cleaned his plate, he put it back on the tray and brushed off crumbs. Only then did he meet her gaze.

"Right, business."

She sipped her tea, eyes still meeting his in a way that made him uncomfortable in the nicest way.

"Emma, I'll have to—"

"Here's the thing. You hired me to do this job. Why?"

"I liked your sense of style. I thought you had a good eye for things."

"Would you say your judgment has often been wrong?"

He thought about it for a moment. "No, can't say that it has."

She met his gaze and held steady. "Trust me now."

It wasn't a question, just a statement delivered with such calm assurance that his insides folded.

"What will you do with the shelf? I'd hate to see it thrown out."

"Oh no, not at all. I have a plan for it in one of the other rooms. You'll see. I would prefer to show you."

"Fine. Now about the jungle in the middle of the house—"

"The terrarium?"

He drained the last bit of coffee from his cup and set it on the tray. His foot had gone to sleep from sitting cross-legged in his work pants. There was a good chance he wouldn't be able to put any weight on it whatsoever. Sneaky girl with her underhanded plans.

"That's too grand a word for such an overgrown mess. I think we should cut our losses and make better use of the space."

Emma flat-stared him. "Give me two days and we'll have this conversation again. Okay?"

"You're fighting me every step of the way."

"You hired me to do a job. I'm doing it." Emma was completely calm, there was no arguing with her.

"Fine. Two days. And you can move the shelf. I'm coming over tonight so we can order furniture online."

Emma grimaced. "I'm sorry, I have plans. Another time, maybe?"

• • • • • • • • •

Emma's plans involved her make-them-in-faith invitations and some chatting to God time. She liked to think of it as a sort-of date night that just happened to be with the God of the entire universe. The thought of it made her happy.

She got out the invitation-making bits and pieces and set them up in the newly finished kitchen. The team had expertly demolished the wall, installed the overhead cabinets and the island countertop. The light that flowed between the two spaces was utterly lovely.

With the kitchen complete, she'd be able to work on her invitations in a beautifully organized space. It was perfect.

She spread out all the bits that went into the invitations and methodically arranged all her tools in a way that she could get to them all. With her heart in her throat, she prayed, speaking her prayers out loud.

"Lord, I hope I'm not wrong about this. I feel like I've heard you so clearly, but I could be wrong." She shook her head. "But you've said that faith is being sure of what we hope for and certain of what we do not see. Right now, I'm not seeing anything between these two, but I'm so sure that they're right for each other. So I'm making these in faith, looking forward to a wedding one day in the future."

As her hands went through the motions, doing the sequence in an almost instinctive way. She prayed as she created the paper that would become their wedding invitations.

"I don't know why this is so important, but I just feel like it is." Her prayers mingled with the petals, the gold flakes, and the bits of torn-up paper.

With expert hands, she guided all the elements to where they needed to be.

Emma was quite lost in the process when she heard a knock on the door.

Chapter Twenty-One

BENEDICT SAT IN THE living room at home. Annoyance brewed over him like a fruit flies over an old peach. This was not how tonight was meant to go down.

Sitting here, by himself in the living room, was not part of his original plan. More than anything, he was bored. Surely Emma wouldn't have plans?

He checked his phone for messages or emails, hoping for a mission that he could go lose himself in for a few hours, but there was nothing.

His mind circled like a vulture and came to settle on the biggest thing that he'd been ignoring for weeks now—the fact that Emma Redwood made him *feel*.

Did he care to investigate those feelings? Nope. Not at all. What a colossal waste of time. Feelings would only trip him up and stop the process that he was working towards.

Falling for Emma was not part of the plan. It was an anomaly that had to be dealt with swiftly and decisively. No way was he entertaining this nonsense. He picked at the issue, turning it over, this way and that.

Like a train approaching in a dark tunnel, a solution began to grow in his mind. What if...

He isolated the thought and analyzed it from all angles. It was risky, but all the best plans were. It might just work.

And! It would solve two problems at once. That was a complete win on every level.

As day slipped into evening and light slowly faded, Benedict sat in the darkness embroidering a plan that would take care of the enigma of Emma and the trouble with Thomas in a neat, clean solution.

There was no denying it. He was a genius.

• • • ● • ● • • •

Emma toyed with the idea of leaving the knocker on the doorstep and simply ignoring whoever it was. Her only plan for the evening was to make invitations and pray. It was after 8 pm and nobody should be knocking at that time of night.

But her conscience demanded that she peep through the spyhole at least.

It was Dani. "Er, do you mind if I come in?"

Emma waved her in with a vague sense of panic. Card makings were all set up on the kitchen table.

"Is something wrong?"

Dani smiled brightly and shook her head but the rate she was blinking told a different tale. "I need tea. I'll make it. Is the kitchen this way?"

Before Emma could stop her, she walked through the house and straight into the kitchen, saw the setup, and asked, "What's all this?"

Emma felt a bit sick. There were two ways she could spin this, be vague or be honest. Sort of.

"I'm making paper." She shrugged and realized she'd opted for both her options rolled into one. Vague honesty.

"What fun. Can I join?" Dani settled onto a stool, studying all the bits laid out.

Emma frowned up at Heaven briefly. "Sure. Why not?" She made tea fighting off weird light-headedness.

She ran Dani through the process.

"Can I try?" Dani looked much happier than when she'd arrived. At Emma's nod, she began swirling elements into the water. Then she kept going, following the steps that Emma had spilled.

"You're a natural. Are you sure you haven't done this before?"

Dani didn't reply, she was so focused on her task. She moved the tray around carefully in the liquid, making sure to catch an even spread of all the elements. When she was done, she lifted it out and pressed the sponge to absorb all the excess liquid.

"So what did you say these were for?" Dani examined her handiwork, turning the tray this way and that. "This is going to be so pretty."

Emma nearly choked on her tongue. Her mind flew to find something she could toss that would throw Dani off track. It wasn't the right time to spill the truth just yet.

Before she could think of what to say, Dani gasped.

"You know what these would be perfect for? Wedding invitations!"

• • • ● • ● • • •

The evening passed quickly filled with gentle laughter as the two girls found a working rhythm.

Dani stood up and stretched, easing out her back. "I feel like I've run a marathon."

"Well, not running, but that was a marathon." Drying rectangles of paper surrounded them. They'd got through far more than Emma could ever have done by herself. Her phone beeped and she checked the message. Of course. Who would message her this time of night, if not Benedict?

Dani stretched forward, hands reaching her toes with ease. "I'm going to the bathroom."

"Sure." Emma waited for her to be out of the room before opening up the message from Benedict.

Benedict: I know this seems a little forward, but would you like to join me for supper tomorrow night? There's a new restaurant opening and I've been invited.

Emma felt a wash of heat through her body. Supper with Benedict. This wasn't their usual business supper that involved food spread out in takeaway boxes and a whole lot of arguing over tile colors and finishes. No, no. This was something other. More like the night in the elevator.

Really, now. Why would the thought of having supper with Benedict make her knees feel weak? It was a warning. That's what. Don't get cozy with the boss. That was a stupid move to be avoided.

Right.

She started to type out *no thanks*, but then realized Dani had been gone a while. She pocketed her phone and went to check on the loo. The door was open with no Dani to be seen. Odd. Holding in her breath, she listened.

The vaguest sound of movement came from the room at the end of the passage. The one that held all of Thomas's paintings. Oh no.

She hurried down the corridor. Lights were on at the end of the hall, and the door to the painting room stood open. Dani was in with the paintings.

Emma rushed into the room, unsure of what she'd find. She hadn't been in since Thomas started here and she had no idea what she was in for.

She stepped into the room and gasped. The image on the easel was of a lion standing majestically on a mound of rock. It was still a work in progress, bits of white shone through in the sunset behind the lion, but something in it snagged her heart. There were other works, too. All animals, clearly for the commission that Thomas had taken on for the restaurant.

Someone sniffed. Dani. She stood on the other side of the room with her hands to her chest and tears running down her cheeks.

"Hey, what's up?" Emma moved in swiftly and stopped when she saw the painting. Completely out of place among all the animal pictures, this one showed a couple hugging. They stood on a mountain top at sunset or sunrise, it was impossible to tell which.

The ocean gleamed in the distance, picking up the light from the sun. Emma could see why it got to Dani, he was in a suit and she was in a poufy white dress with a soft veil blowing on the gentle breeze. The wedding theme was painfully obvious.

Dani dashed away her tears, but they were instantly replaced with new ones.

"Sorry. I don't know what came over me." She waved at her face as if she could fan away the tears.

Emma was still feeling weirdly fuzzy from the message from Benedict, but she shoved all those feelings into a corner, they didn't mean anything, anyway. She focused all her attention on her friend who was sobbing, gulping down air in between sobs.

Emma put her arm around Dani to comfort her.

"Come on, let's get you out of here and you can tell me what's going on."

Dani didn't fight, she let Emma lead her away from the painting, throwing backward glances as they left the room.

It was only after nibbling her way through a chocolate cappuccino muffin (that Emma feared she'd choke on) and two cups of coffee that Dani's tearful sobbing calmed down enough for her to talk.

"Here's the thing, I don't know why Thomas broke up with me. I thought we were great together." She shrugged and looked so delicate in that moment, Emma feared she might start crying again.

"What did he say?" Emma dipped a toe into the conversation she'd been longing to have since the first day she met the girl.

"He was very nice about it all. It was *him, not me*. That he wouldn't be able to give me the life I deserve." Dani broke off staring at her empty mug to frown at Emma. "What does that mean, anyway?"

"Did he have a job?" Emma tried to ignore the teensy sparks of excitement. If income was the big issue here, that was all about to change.

"He dabbled here and there, he always seemed to have money for whatever he needed, he mentioned something about a trust fund. I don't think he had a steady job. No." She sighed and put down her cup as a gloomy resolution settled on her face. "I guess this is my funeral cry."

"Dani? What on earth are you talking about?"

"You know. You cry at a funeral as you're saying goodbye to someone, then it's over. You move on. Tomorrow, I'll move on."

Emma panicked. "Not so fast. I want to hear more. What do you like about the guy?"

"Are we honestly going to do this? I should get home and let you get on with whatever it is you do when you're not painting rocks."

"Do you really want to go back to your apartment with that charming roommate of yours?"

Dani swallowed so hard, Emma heard it. "No, no I don't. Could I stay with you? I can sleep on a couch. I don't snore. At least I don't think I do."

"Good, I love that plan. Now, I'm making tea and you're going to tell me what you like about Thomas. Deal?"

• • • • ● • ● • • •

It was long after midnight when Benedict's phone blipped to life with a message from Emma. So the girl had said yes to supper. A strange feeling crept over him, like getting goosebumps from an orchestra crescendo, yet deeper and more satisfying.

Maybe he should just forget the plan and enjoy supper with her? Even as he thought it, he knew there was no way he could entertain that idea. He had to go with the plan. It was better for everybody.

Chapter Twenty-Two

EMMA WOKE UP TO the sound of dishes clinking in the kitchen. Her heart raced as her brain tried to surface through the thick fog of sleep. Her dreams had been a mixed-up business of Benedict eating supper sitting cross-legged on the lounge floor while telling her about funerals. With the man so strongly on her mind, she couldn't help thinking he might be in the kitchen.

Dani. Dani had slept over. She was in the kitchen, not Benedict. Emma stayed in the warmth of her duvet, rolled onto her back, and saw Legs on the ceiling above her. The small spider seemed to notice her attention and scurried off to disappear behind a hole in the cornice.

"Thanks for leaving, buddy." Emma didn't hate the spider anymore, but the thought of it dropping on her made her twitchy. That would end badly for one of them.

Her mind sifted through the progress of the night before. Dani had spoken about Thomas for over an hour solid. It was clear that she knew the man inside out, back to front and back again. Not only did she know him, but she loved him deeply.

Emma hoped it was enough.

She slid her feet into slippers and was about to shuffle through to the kitchen when she thought about her PJs. She'd thought they were cute when she bought them, grey with pink bunnies. Now, they were 8 years old and not so cute anymore.

It took a few minutes to find shorts and a strappy blouse that always made her feel summery. She didn't bother to find shoes but headed to the kitchen barefoot.

The countertop was set for breakfast.

Dani grinned at her. "I hope you don't mind. I've just cut up fruit for muesli, and made some toast, and tea."

Emma sat down and spooned fruit into her bowl. The yogurt was thick and laced with honey.

"This is great. I'd usually just swallow a cup of coffee and be done." She stirred a spoon of sugar into her tea and wondered whether she should bring up the subject of Thomas's brother. She took a deep breath and stepped off the cliff.

"You haven't said much about Thomas's brother. Talk to me."

Dani looked puzzled. "Benedict? Why?"

Emma avoided her eyes. "No reason. I was just wondering if there's something more than a typical meddling big brother."

Dani wasn't taking her bait.

"He just seems to have so many secrets and I can't decide if there are legitimate things that he's keeping quiet about, or if he's just got some grand savior complex going on." She grabbed her teacup and took a deep drink, all the while peering at Dani over the top of the rim.

Dani frowned and poked at the fruit in her bowl with a spoon. "He's an enigma. But I always got the impression that he was a good guy. I don't think he would have done anything bad?" Her head shot up and she stared at Emma. "Do you think he would have?"

"I don't know him well enough to say. I was just wondering. It's a common thing. Meddling big brothers."

A worried frown had settled in between Dani's eyebrows. "I'll think about it and let you know."

• • • ● • ● • • •

Emma fiddled with her skirt wondering if she should have worn something different. She loved the feel of this skirt as it swished around her ankles in a soft froth. The blouse she'd paired it with was a delicate shade of pink that picked up on the flowers in the skirt. It was a combination that made her feel pretty.

But she was having supper with Benedict, her boss. Maybe a three-piece power suit would have been a better choice.

Either way, it was too late. His car had just pulled up in the driveway.

Emma's tummy flipped at the sight of him getting out of the car. He wore dark pants and a white shirt, open at the neck, with the sleeves rolled back. Emma breathed deep and tried to squish all the butterflies that flocked inside of her but she simply couldn't.

She jumped at the sound of the doorbell. *Honestly Emma, get a grip.*

His eyes flicked over her as she opened the door.

"You ready? I've made reservations."

Words spilled out of Emma as they drove through the quiet streets. Something about paint and new faucets for the kitchen, and a loose tile on the kitchen backsplash. He said nothing and she had to wonder if he'd heard a single word she'd said.

"Are you even listening to me?"

He blinked once. "You need new undercoating for the living room, the faucet in the kitchen needs to be replaced, and the kitchen backsplash has a wonky tile." He flashed her a quick grin. "Does that about cover it?"

"Pretty much." Emma breathed deeply to calm her heart rate. This was a bad idea, supper with this man. Or maybe it wasn't.

The restaurant they pulled up to was a shimmering oasis in the inky blackness of the cool night. It glimmered demurely, tempting people to come inside. Four Nations Food offered a concept she'd been interested in for a while, a chance to sample the cuisine from four different countries all in one evening.

Benedict tucked her hand over his arm and led the way into the building. The staff scurried when they saw him, leaving one waiter who bowed low.

"Follow me, sir. Your table is right this way."

• • • ● • ● • • •

Benedict led Emma to the table they'd booked for him with his insides churning. All he had to do was stick to the plan and it would all work out. That's what plans were for. Sticking to them was the best way to avoid nonsense.

Right.

Then why did he have the overwhelming urge to bail on the plan? He snuck a glance at Emma. Her blonde hair brushed over her shoulders and fell forward catching the light. She tucked it behind her ears without thinking and breathed slowly.

She looked so pretty in what she was wearing. But then again, she looked pretty in dungarees too. She could probably wear a hessian sack and still look pretty.

He brought himself up sharply. Focus!

With a sigh, he shoved aside all the thoughts that mushroomed trying to convince him to cancel the plan. He was stronger than that.

He avoided the temptation to sit on his hands. He was in control, for crying out loud.

"So why supper? Are we celebrating something I don't know about?" Emma's eyes sparkled and he wanted to run his fingers through her hair.

"Does there have to be a special occasion for a meal out?" He kept his voice pitched low and it worked. He sounded mostly unaffected.

"Come on, Benedict. I know you better than this. You're my boss. We don't just have dinner together. Should I have brought my laptop?"

It was as if someone had cranked up the intensity on his senses. Her voice sent a shiver through him. Ridiculous!

"Most definitely not. We'll get back to that tomorrow."

A hint of a smile touched her lips. *Don't look at her lips.* Emma's skin glowed in the flickering candlelight. He shut his eyes to block out the sight. He reached for his phone to send a message and as he did, he heard Thomas's voice.

"Hi. Oh, who do we have here?"

Benedict's heart sank. He was too late. The plan was now in motion, there was no pulling back or stopping now. He took a moment to feel the sting, then folded all the feelings up until were small enough to ignore.

"Thomas, I'd like you to meet Emma. Emma, this is Thomas."

• • • • ● • ● • • •

Emma felt heat wash through her at the sight of Benedict's brother. She panicked. Benedict couldn't find out that she and Thomas knew each other. That would cause nothing but problems.

While Benedict seemed preoccupied trying to catch the attention of the waitress, Emma stretched her eyes wide at Thomas and mouthed *what are you doing here?*

His eyes slid sideways to Benedict. Emma pointed at the man, then held her palms up. *What do you mean?*

At that moment Benedict swung back to face them and both their faces switched to vacant grins.

"Emma here is working for me and Thomas is—"

"The baby brother." Thomas shot the words in quickly and winked at Emma with the eye that Benedict couldn't see.

Benedict rubbed his chin, a thoughtful look on his face. "That's one way of putting it, I suppose."

A waitress stopped at their table. "Can I take your drinks order?"

Benedict pulled out his phone, checked his messages, and said, "Oh no. Will you look at that? Unfortunately, I need to go. So sorry to dump and run. But you know what? Why don't you two feel stay on here and order whatever you want? The bill is taken care of."

Emma felt a hole opening up under her feet. "Where are you going? I thought we were going to have supper?"

"Change of plans. Thomas here is good company. Enjoy. Oh, try the crab meat starter. It's delicious." His chair scraped loudly on the floor as he left, leaving Emma and Thomas staring at each other across a candlelit table.

Thomas was frowning. "What's going on here?"

"You tell me. He's your brother."

"Did this feel planned to you?" Thomas stared out the window where he could see Benedict climbing into his car. "This feels very planned to me. What did he say to you? About coming here tonight?"

Emma thought back over the message and a feeling washed over her that left her hollowed out. Benedict wasn't interested in her at all, it was all just a setup with his brother.

"I thought it was, er, just a business supper."

Thomas took a sip of water from Emma's glass. "You don't mind, hey?" He took another deep swig.

Emma sighed. "Finish it, it's fine."

"You look a little put out. Have you maybe fallen for the man's charms?"

"Don't be daft. I just don't like it when plans change. I like things to be more predictable. Another thing that bothers me is not knowing what he wants to achieve with this." She waved her hand at the space between them. "I don't get it."

Thomas leaned back in his chair with his eyes shut. "I do. You're a beautiful girl, he wants me to get over my ex. There's no reason we shouldn't fall madly in love and leave here with a brand new destiny." His eyes flicked open and he caught her gaze. "Right?"

A small spark of rage shot off in Emma's stomach. "On paper, yes. I'll admit that you would check a good number of boxes on my list. But—"

"You have a list?" They paused for a moment while the waitress placed food on their table, fussed a bit with rearranging the various bottles of condiments and spices before finally leaving.

"Of course." Emma eyed him with suspicion. "Don't you?"

Thomas thought for a bit. "I guess I do. It's pretty short though."

"Really? What's on it?" She sat forward in her chair, keen to hear what he was going to say next.

A bleak look crept over his face. He almost looked green. With the biggest sigh she'd heard coming from him, he breathed, "Dani."

At that moment, he looked so sad, Emma felt a stab of pain in her heart for him. For Dani, for both of them. She reached over to take his hand to comfort him. "I'm so sorry Thomas. Maybe it doesn't have to be over. Think about it."

"Oh but it is. I made sure of that. I didn't just burn the bridge, I crucified the engineers who built it."

"Thomas?" As if summoned by her name, Dani appeared. She stared from one to the other, blinking too fast. Her eyes came to rest on Emma's hand, still holding Thomas's. "I didn't know you two knew each other. I ... I have to go."

Emma pulled her hand back as if Thomas's skin was on fire. "Dani! Wait. This isn't what you're thinking." Her words fell to the ground and the other people in the restaurant turned to stare.

Thomas pushed away from the table. "I'm going after her." He was halfway out the restaurant when he turned back, "I'm sorry—"

"Thomas! Go! She's getting away. Run! I'll be praying."

He took off like a spooked deer and the restaurant door slammed shut behind him. At that moment the waitress arrived with three full plates of food. Emma buried her face in her hands and groaned. What a mess.

"Should I package these meals up as take-aways?"

Emma thought she might throw up. "Sure." Her heart shredded at the thought of how Dani must be feeling. This was a disaster. A huge, horrific, disaster and she had nobody to blame but herself.

Chapter Twenty-Three

It was early morning, a bit early for their usual meeting, but Benedict was eager to hear what had happened the night before. With any luck, Thomas and Emma had connected nicely over dinner and had realized just how compatible they were.

He was a good guy and she was, well, Emma. With her soft heart and sparkling eyes. She was irresistible. There was no doubt in his mind that he'd done the right thing. He ignored the sting in his own heart, he was tough, this pain would pass.

He knocked on the door and paced the porch for about a minute until impatience got the best of him. Using the spare key, he let himself in and went through to the kitchen to put the kettle on.

The backsplash they'd argued over had been completed and, he had to admit, Emma was right. The pale mint offset the sandstone in a way that was both classy and elegant.

He checked his watch. Usually, by now, Emma would have come bustling through with thirty questions and a list of things as long as his left leg for him to approve. It was odd that she hadn't yet.

He heard water running deeper in the house and decided to investigate. Listening carefully, his ears led him to the terrarium that he fully intended to tear down. The door was open and he walked in. Was that the sound of running water?

He moved fast. Leaks caused damage and they couldn't afford a setback. He ran in and stopped dead. The place was no longer overgrown with weeds but felt like a tropical jungle. Across the path up ahead, he saw the source of the trickling.

He'd forgotten about the natural stream that ran below the house and made an appearance here in the terrarium. It had been blocked up for as long as he could remember, but now it ran freely, bubbling through the room unhindered, making music as it ran swiftly over rocks and swirled in pools.

The pathway ran over a wooden bridge and into a space that was vibrantly alive. He'd never seen this place so awake. Not even when his mom tended it.

His feet led him forwards and he moved slowly as if a fast movement might just shatter the illusion and it would all be gone. The path led through the tamed jungle, with dappled shades of green off-setting the brightly colored flowers that filled the air with their scent.

He nearly fell over backward at the sight of a low tent pitched on the rug in the middle of the room. It was one of those that popped up easily and didn't need tent pegs to hold its shape. The rustling sounds he'd heard came from inside.

"Emma?"

"Hmm?" It was Emma and she sounded like she was still mostly asleep.

"Did you just spend the night in a tent?"

Emma peered through the doorway opening just enough so her eyes and nose poked through. "You're early." Her face was all scrunched up.

"Not that early. Why are you sleeping in a tent?"

The tent flap snapped shut with a hard flick of canvas and her voice drifted his way through the fabric. "What do you care?"

"I'm in the kitchen making coffee when you're ready."

She pushed her way out of the tent with a dressing gown thrown over what looked like gray pajamas with some small animals printed on them. "Oh, I'm ready to hear exactly what you were thinking last night. Why would you pull a stunt like that?"

"A stunt like what? I don't see the problem." Her hair was sticking up in all directions and her eyes were bloodshot. He just wanted to hug her. "This place looks incredible."

"Don't change the subject. You set me up with your brother and left. What were you thinking?"

"Emma, you make it sound so bad. Honestly, I thought you could both do with a good night of conversation. Maybe get to know each other a little better. Why are you angry?"

Emma leaned on her forearms with a smile he'd come to recognize as trouble. "What do you think? The icing on the cake was organizing Dani to come past. How on earth did you get that right? It was very impressive. I know you want to sabotage their relationship, but that was all a bit rich."

"Dani?" He'd never seen her so sarcastic. "Why would Dani show up at that place?"

Emma said nothing, just stared at him with eyebrows lifted.

"Look, it doesn't matter. They are history anyway. How did you and Thomas get on?" Surely it couldn't have been a complete train wreck?

Emma spooned coffee into their mugs with such force some of the coffee kernels bounced out onto the countertop. She smiled at him and he knew he was in trouble. "He's great. A great guy. Wonderful."

"Look, I get that you're angry. I do. But just tell me one thing, why the tent?"

Emma met his glance with a blank stare. "I'm sorry, I have work to do. If there's anything else you'd like to discuss, I'll be in the guest toilet."

Benedict watched Emma leave and resisted the urge to scratch his head. How could his great plan have blown up like this? If Emma was fuming, Thomas would be beyond livid.

He sipped his coffee and thought about the one question that he just wasn't getting answers for. Why the tent?

• • • • ● • ● • • •

Emma chipped off broken tiles feeling the satisfying clattering smash as they hit the ground.

She'd decided to skip going to rock painting under the excuse of needing the finish things here in the house.

Truthfully, the thought of facing Dani filled her with a deep dread. Thomas hadn't messaged to say what had happened. He may have caught up and been able to convince her of the truth, or he may not have. Frankly, Emma was too scared to ask.

As if overhearing her thoughts, her phone blipped. It was a message from Brenda.

Brenda: Don't make me come fetch you.

Aah, the ever-charming Brenda. Emma toyed with the idea of ignoring her but she had the feeling Brenda may well hunt her down and drag her there. She was *that* level of scary.

After a quick shower, Emma threw on a red shirt and her favorite pair of dungarees and drove across town wishing she were braver.

She climbed the stairs expecting to see the old crew and no Dani. To her surprise, Dani was there, sitting next to the only open seat in the studio. Her heart sank as she walked closer, mind running wild with what she should say.

Dani looked up and smiled. Not a fake smile either, but an honest smile with openness in her eyes.

Emma cleared her throat. "About the last night..."

Dani put a hand on her arm. "No worries. Thomas managed to catch me. He told me everything."

Emma could barely hear over the rush of blood to her ears. "And?"

Dani shot a glance toward where Brenda sat at the front, presiding over the room. "We must chat, but for now, we'd better just paint rocks." Her eyes flicked sideways and Emma understood.

"So we're all good?"

"Of course." Dani grinned at her briefly before turning her attention to the rock in front of her. She whispered softly, so only Emma caught it, "Better than good."

Emma had so many questions. How much did Thomas explain? How much did Dani know about who Emma truly was? Considering that Thomas didn't even know who she was in the first place, she doubted that Dani would have a real clue.

Brenda clapped her hands to get their attention. "Right ladies, we are working towards our next batch for planting. Let's see some great work please."

Emma glanced over to what Dani was painting and blinked back tears. A glorious sunrise splashed across her rock with the words *there is always hope* nestled in the sunlit clouds.

• • • ● • ● • • •

Thomas was up and eating breakfast when Benedict came downstairs just after 6 a.m.

"Are you sick? Why are you up?"

Thomas swallowed a mouthful of coffee and shrugged. "You don't have dibs on early mornings."

Maybe he'd get to find out more about last night from Thomas. Dani showing up was the opposite of what last night was meant to achieve. Although, if she'd got the wrong idea, that could work in their favor.

"Fair enough. How did last night work out?"

"Considering I thought we were going to have a brotherly catch-up? Not what I was expecting, but other than that, remarkably well."

Benedict frowned. "Oh brilliant." He cleared his throat and dropped the enthusiasm a few notches. "Would you want to have a bro catch up?"

Thomas put down his spoon, lifted the bowl to his lips, and drained the milk. He put down the bowl and regarded Benedict as he licked the milk off his lips, just the way a five-year-old would. "Before last night, I was keen. Now? I'm not actually sure. I do have a question though, did you have a genuine emergency, or was that all planned?"

His attitude gave Benedict an uncomfortable feeling, like the time he touched a poison ivy knowing full well what it was and suffered through the rash for days.

"You know I can't talk about my job. Subject change. We need to talk about you earning a living. You need a job."

Thomas stared him straight in the eye. "You know what? *I* can't talk about *my* job."

Benedict stared at his baby brother at a loss for words. He had no idea how to respond.

Thomas laughed. "You should see your face right now. Priceless. Seriously though, it's covered. Chill." Thomas refilled his bowl and scooped up another spoonful of cereal. He still ate the sugar-laced, chocolate-flavored crunchy flakes.

"Why do you still eat that? You're not five anymore. It's pure sugar."

"Try some. I dare you." Thomas slid an empty bowl across the table and pushed the box of cereal closer too.

"Dude, I'm not eating that." Benedict sat on the chair opposite Thomas. He couldn't get the image of the tent and the terrarium out of his head. He couldn't understand it. "I have a question for you."

"Oh no please, not another one." Thomas looked ready to grab his bowl and bolt.

"Not about you, don't worry. It's about girls."

"You're asking *me* for girl advice?"

"Oh shoosh. I haven't been in a relationship in a seriously long time, I'm not sure I remember how those things are meant to work. Besides, it's not really about a relationship, more about how women think."

"Sure. Fire away."

There was no way to say this without sounding like a crazy person. "Why would a girl pitch a tent inside and sleep in it, rather than in a perfectly good bed?"

"Oh! Well, that happens all the time."

"Really? I had no idea. What does it mean?"

"Benedict, I'm joking. That's pretty weird. Who's doing that?" It took a glare from Benedict to get him to drop the question. "Keep your secrets. I think I get it."

Benedict flat-stared his brother. This whole thing had thrown him off balance. He hated it. Being so unstable was simply not a good way to live. "Obviously if it's weird, you'd understand it. You're like the poster-child of weirdness."

Thomas accepted that with a humble nod. "True, true. You're not wrong. Now do you want my opinion or not?"

Benedict waved a hand. *Bring it on.*

"I would say, the girl in question doesn't feel at home in the place she's staying. The tent is a bid to carve out her own space. To make someplace feel like home. Something about wherever she's staying is making her feel unsafe. That's just a guess though. Without knowing who you're talking about, I can't say for sure."

Benedict mulled over his words, weighing them up.

"Here, have some of this." Thomas poured some chocolate cereal into the bowl he'd given Benedict earlier. "It will help you think."

Benedict said nothing but took the bowl and shoved a spoonful in his mouth. The sweetness of the sugar hit his tongue and he forced himself to chew and swallow. By the third mouthful, he barely noticed the sweetness.

Thomas pushed back from the table. "It's been fun, but I've got to get out of here. I won't be home for supper, so don't worry about me."

Benedict watched him go as he ate the last bit of cereal. It wasn't that bad once you got used to it. His mind turned one question over, poking at it and examining it from every angle. Why did Emma not feel safe? What was he doing wrong?

Chapter Twenty-Four

THE GROUP HAD PRODUCED a tidy pile of rocks for their evening's work. Brenda looked at their haul and nodded once. "Good job, ladies. We have enough to go planting. How does tomorrow night sound for you all?"

Dani elbowed Emma. "Should we do it?

Emma was dying to know how things were between Dani and Thomas and if it took a rock planting session that she had no energy for to find out, she was in.

"I wouldn't miss it."

Dani looked happy. Emma checked her watch. "I think we've got time to do another one or two each."

Dani didn't hesitate. She grabbed the biggest rock from the pile, slapped on a base coat of deep green, mottled a white pattern on the surface using a damp sponge, and let it dry. Then she took a skinny paintbrush and carefully painted the words *you are worth more than you believe you are* in a gracefully flowing script.

She blew on the paint to dry it, then turned the rock over and painted a contact number.

The rocks Emma painted lately were all intricate and moody. Dani seemed to have transitioned as every single one of hers had an encouraging message and a phone number on the back.

"Whose phone number is that? I hope it's not yours." Emma had always thought the girl too trusting.

"Oh no, it's a counseling service that I volunteer at. It's run by some of the people in my church."

"Wait, are you a Believer?" Emma's heart skipped.

"I am! You?" Dani's face was glowing.

Emma found breathing hard and she nodded. "What's your favorite Bible verse?"

Dani thought for a moment, then she said, "Hebrews eleven, verse one."

Emma wanted to laugh. "Now faith is being sure of what we hope for and certain of what do not see. Right?"

"Yes. You know it. The version I like says 'faith is the substance of things hoped for, the evidence of things not seen.'"

Emma blinked back tears. This was one of those rare moments where the fabric of heaven and earth met under the gentle pressure of God's loving hand. "One day remind me to tell you the story behind that verse."

Dani looked puzzled. "Sure." She didn't push but left Emma to brood over the wonder of the mystery by herself. "We should each paint one with that verse on. Don't you think?"

Emma turned back to her half-done cat. "Good idea. Let me finish this little guy and I'll do mine."

By the time Emma was done her cat and started on her verse rock, Dani was finished. "That was quick."

Dani shrugged. "I knew exactly what I wanted to do. I think I'm done for the night. I'll see you tomorrow night. Should I meet you in the park?"

"Great. That's a good plan." Emma kept her tone light, but she was still freaked out by the fact that Dani hadn't told exactly what had happened last night.

The same restlessness stewed inside for the rest of the evening and the whole of the next day. Emma almost cried with relief when it was time to go to the park.

Dani was still upbeat and they headed into the park where they'd be planting the current batch. After a brief discussion over who was going where all the ladies disappeared in opposite directions.

"Come this way, I know a nice place." Dani led the way to a quiet part of the park. They both planted rocks as they went, but it all happened at a much faster pace than Emma was used to.

Dani was on a mission. She didn't stop for each rock plant, merely slowed enough to give them each a few seconds to place a rock then she kept walking.

Emma followed without questioning it, but her curiosity was off the charts. Dani hadn't taken the lead once in all the times they'd come out rock planting. Why she felt the need to do it now and at such a speed, was a mystery.

They skirted around the edge of a wide duck pond and found a coffee shop that Emma didn't know existed.

Dani grinned at her. "C'mon."

Emma got the distinct feeling that this was all planned when she followed Dani in and found none other than Thomas sitting at a table reading through a menu.

She sat down not sure what to expect. Dani slid in next to Thomas who gave her a quick hug and kissed her cheek.

"Guys, I'm so happy for you. But why am I here?"

Thomas and Dani shared a look.

Thomas spoke up. "I'm worried about my brother. Whatever secret thing he's involved in is going to get him into trouble. I don't know anything for sure, I just have a really bad feeling."

Dani nodded and patted Thomas's leg in agreement then turned to Emma. "We want to stage an intervention and we want you to help us."

Chapter Twenty-Five

BENEDICT CHECKED THE PLAN for the week. He had one extraction planned for Friday and the house he had lined up was all ready and due to be cleaned by Tuesday. The crew would come in and kit it out by Thursday and he'd deliver the family on Friday. Perfect.

He was not intending to check on Emma this week, the girl had her plan for the week and just had to keep going the way she was and they'd stay on track. He wanted to give her some time to think about how great Thomas was.

She'd be good for him. Dani was a sweet girl, but she was studying to work in social welfare which wasn't exactly one of the most highly paid jobs. Thomas needed someone who could inspire him to get moving and Emma was, if nothing else, inspiring.

With that all neatly tucked away—

A message came through on his phone.

COR Crew: The project timeline for the Sapphire extraction has escalated. Finish the house within two weeks. Life and death.

The Sapphire extraction was the house that Emma was working on. She was on track to finish in two months, not two weeks. His mind scrambled to find an alternative plan, but everything he thought of wouldn't work.

He was going to have to go see Emma immediately.

• • • ● • ● • ● • • •

Emma had a contractor in to redo the plumbing in the guest bathroom. The pipework was still good, but the toilet and basin were old and damaged. There were some strange chips in the toilet bowl that she couldn't imagine how they'd got there.

She'd just boiled water for a well-earned cup of tea when Benedict arrived looking a little thunderous.

"I didn't expect to see you this week. What's up?"

"We've got a slight problem."

"Like the strange hole in the toilet seat. Have you seen that thing? I have no idea what would cause a mark like that."

"Probably a firecracker."

"How would you know that?" She eyed him, giving him an opportunity to admit he'd grown up in this house, but he barely noticed.

"Boys do things like that." He eyed her sideways with a small shrug.

She pulled out another cup and fixed him tea just the way he liked it. With another look at his face, she put a freshly baked slice of lemon meringue on a plate and slid both towards him.

The tension on his face eased as he ate a mouthful. He chewed and swallowed in silence while Emma watched him closely, trying to guess what the *slight problem* could be and how he'd take to having an intervention done on him. She had a feeling it would not end well, but Thomas and Dani were determined.

He almost put the plate down, but changed his mind and finished his slice in another two bites. By the time he was ready to talk, Emma felt like ants were crawling beneath her skin.

"So here's the thing. Our original timeframe has been shortened. This house has to be done in two weeks."

He had to be joking, there was no way that was possible. Emma put on her best game face. "Oh sure, no problem at all. I don't know why we didn't move the deadline up ourselves." She ended with a laugh, slapping her thigh to show her amusement. Benedict made jokes. Who knew?

"I'm not kidding, Emma. But I have a plan."

Emma felt his words sink into her. Not only was her job nearly over, but she also had two weeks to find a new place to live. She felt like crying. Of all the turmoil going through her mind, one word made it out through her lips. "Why?"

"The need for the house has become urgent. But don't worry, I have a plan."

"Two weeks."

He nodded and pulled out his laptop. "I've worked out if we drop some of the *nice to have's* and go with pure essentials, we can probably get it done in time. It would mean that I move into the house with you, we can run double teams. Either that or work around the clock, I'll take the evening crew and you work with a daytime bunch."

"You want to move in here."

Benedict nodded. "It's the only way. We've got to get this done."

Emma folded her arms. "I don't know how I feel about that."

"There's nothing to be afraid of. I'm not dangerous." He met her eyes coolly. "Not really."

Emma's heart pounded in her chest. Something burned in his eyes she didn't dare identify. In amongst all the insecurity over her future, all the turmoil this man had caused in the last five minutes, all Emma could think of was what it would be like to be taken into his arms and thoroughly kissed. Oh, he was dangerous, very, very, dangerous.

She cleared her throat and forced herself to look out the window. The roses she'd trimmed were covered in green shoots. Pruning worked wonders if you knew what you were doing.

He reached for her hand across the countertop. Warmth flooded through her as his skin met hers. "Emma, it's an emergency. We have to get this done. It's the only way. I'm not here to harm you."

His words washed over her and she felt her equilibrium leave, sucked away by a maelstrom of emotions that bubbled up out of nowhere.

"At least can you tell me what the emergency is?" She threw out the question as a test.

"You know I can't do that." He sighed. "Look, if you're not comfortable with me in the house, I'll pitch a tent in the front yard or something. You'll just have to let me in to use the bathroom."

"Fine. That sounds like a plan."

"I was joking, but I guess if that would work for you, I can."

She took in his broad shoulders, the intensity of his brown eyes, and the hair that she just wanted to run her fingers through. "It's the only way."

A vague frown settled into his eyebrows. "Fine. I'll make arrangements." He stared at her for a moment before turning his attention to the spreadsheet of their new timeline.

A thought occurred to Emma and it put a smile on her face that she couldn't shake. This meant that he was going to have to open up the locked cellar.

He looked up and caught her grinning. "Why are you smiling?"

She tried to reverse the grin, but it wouldn't budge. "Nothing. Nothing at all."

• • • • • • • • • •

Benedict finished with Emma and left her making phone calls to line up the orders and contractors they'd need to pull off this miracle over the next two weeks. He went tent shopping. But the weather was changing and he had no real desire to be living under canvas in the winds that would be blowing in.

He left the store empty-handed and went home to pack. Thomas was home, making himself a chicken sandwich.

"Why do you look so miserable?" Thomas asked before taking a big bite out of his lunch.

"I hate wind. Listen, I won't be here for the next two weeks. Will you be fine by yourself?"

Thomas was silently mouthing the word *wind* to himself with a puzzled look on his face. "Sure. Where will you be?"

"Just a project I'm working on. I need to live in a tent for two weeks." He groaned and rubbed a hand across his face. "I'm too old for this."

"Sounds like an adventure to me." Thomas laughed. He seemed lighter as if years of stress had lifted off him. "I know someone with a camper van if you'd like me to ask?"

Benedict stopped short. "Right now that feels like you're handing me a get out of jail free card. That would be better. Not amazing, but better."

Thomas winked at his brother and got on the phone. Within minutes it was all organized.

Benedict felt a wave of gratitude pass through him. "This helps me. Thank you. I don't often have help in the line of work I'm in."

Chapter Twenty-Six

EMMA WAS OUT HANGING washing, hoping to *not* spot Invisible James the security guard by accident (he'd be mortified all over again) when she heard the driveway gate rattle open and something big roll into the yard. Her first thought was moving vehicles and she panicked. Leaving a shirt half-hung, she ran around the side of the house, through the rose garden to the front where she was greeted with the biggest camper van she'd ever seen. It parked in a secluded section of the garden.

Benedict's car pulled up in the driveway and he climbed out looking rather pleased with himself.

"Behold! My tent."

"That's *not* a tent."

"It means I'm not sleeping in the house with you, I think it qualifies." It was the first time she'd seen him in a t-shirt and it threw her to see him in anything other than formal wear.

"It's going to kill that patch of lawn. You do realize this, right?"

"I think the people who need this house won't mind if the grass isn't perfect."

Before she could ask him to elaborate, he moved on, changing the topic so fast, Emma's head spun.

"Are you ready to move some mountains, dear Emma?"

Emma, who still needed to wash her face and drag a brush through her hair was most definitely *not* ready to move mountains.

He didn't wait for a response, but slung an arm around her shoulder and marched her inside. He smelled of shower soap and guy deodorant and underneath it all, a trace of something uniquely Benedict that she couldn't put her finger on.

It overwhelmed her senses and she ducked out from underneath his arm to hang onto her sanity. "Coffee?"

Safely in the kitchen, she splashed water on her face and breathed deeply, trying to calm her emotions. It was all too much. He was unsettling, but the worst of it all was the thought of being homeless again in two weeks.

In through the nose, out through the mouth. Just breathe. God has a plan, don't panic. Have some faith.

In through the—

"What's going on here? Do you need help?"

No! She was not going to cry. This place didn't feel like home anyway. Did it? She controlled her face to careful composure and turned around to *I'm fine* Benedict, but instead of being a safe distance away, he was right up close with a worried look on his face that she'd never been on the receiving end of before. It almost undid her.

"I think I know what's bugging you."

"I just need my first cup of tea and I'll be fine." The only way to stop herself from giving in to the warmth of his closeness was to glare at him, so she glared.

"Mm." He said nothing more but took her favorite cup down and fixed her tea just the way she liked it. He made toast, cut slices of cheese, and melted it in the microwave. "You need to eat."

"How did you know—" she waved towards the toast and tea. He'd got it just as she liked it.

"In my line of work, it pays to be observant."

"Observant house-flipping." She followed him through to the main bedroom which was due to be painted. "I don't know, Benedict. There's more to it than that. What are you not telling me?"

"There are many things I'm not about to tell you. But let's talk about this bedroom. I want it to feel like a safe space. What color do you suggest?" He trailed off and jogged over to stare up at the ceiling.

"There's a spider here, let me take care of him quick." Benedict glanced at her feet. "Pass me your shoe."

"That's Legs. Don't kill him, he's been good company."

He stared at her with a look on his face that spoke eloquently of her dubious state of mind. "You are friends with a spider. Emma. Dear Emma. You need to get out more."

Emma dismissed his concern with a shrug and took a bite of toast. As she did, a strange thought hit her. It had been a very long time since she'd eaten something that she didn't cook herself. The thought made her nose sting.

She retreated to the topic of safe colors. "I don't know that you get safe colors. It's probably different for every person. For this room, I'm thinking peach."

"Peach?"

"Pale peach, yes." She'd shot up a quick prayer for the person who'd be living there and felt the gentle settling in her soul. "Without a doubt."

"Peach it is then."

• • • ● • ● • ● • •

It was misty outside and the sun was yet to show up when Benedict took Emma her first cup of tea of the day. He crossed the bridge into her tiny patch of paradise and wished tents came with doorbells. The stubborn girl insisted on staying in her tent.

"Em, here's tea." He set it down outside her tent flap and stretched to wake himself up. The skylights overhead were all deep gray, as if the sky were sulking.

The change in this vast room still shocked him. This room had been so dead in his eyes, he would have bulldozed it without a thought. But Emma saw deeper than he did. She saw life even though every outward sign said otherwise. Then she stubbornly set her mind to coax life back into every leaf and tree.

It still shook him to the core to realize how big his blind spot was. What else was he wrong about? It made him twitchy to think about.

He'd been rescuing people for so long, the pure cruelty he faced every day was getting to him. He was doing what he could to make life better for each family, but it wasn't enough. He felt like the little guy throwing stranded starfish back into the ocean. The only problem was that he wasn't the little boy saying *it matters to this one*, but rather the cynic looking at the millions still stranded and declaring failure. No matter how hard he worked, there was a beach full of those he couldn't rescue.

It wasn't enough.

He wasn't enough.

That thought ate at him. Recognizing it didn't make it feel better.

As he watched, a single sunray broke the horizon. At first, the dull gray persisted, but light proved irresistible and the rays flooded the sky in deep orange with pinkish tinges, driving back the gloom and transforming the sky.

Benedict felt his heart lift at the sight but it soon slipped back to gray and he knew he was right. Not enough.

• • • • ● • ● • • •

Emma was inspecting the new linen cupboard when she heard Benedict call.

"Emma! I'm ready for you. Come on down." He'd set up his laptop on the kitchen counter and was drumming his fingers on the granite top.

Emma popped into the kitchen looking slightly harassed. They'd been working around the clock for three days now, and could probably count the number of hours they'd both slept on one hand.

"What do you need me for?" She wiped her hands off on her denim pants.

"We're buying furniture. We've got to get the order in today so that they can deliver before this week."

Emma swallowed hard. She hadn't found a place to live yet. She sat next to him without thinking and flinched when their legs brushed.

He didn't seem to notice, but focused on the screen to click on a drop-down menu that said *bedroom furniture*.

Something had been bothering Emma. As they sat and waited for the website to load, she remembered. "Oh, by the way. There's an unpainted patch of wall in the peach room. Did you get tired or something?"

Benedict didn't miss a beat. "Legs was chilling there, I didn't want to bother the little guy. Don't worry about it, I'll go finish off when we're done here." He faced her with his eyebrows lifted. "Focus now, we're going to choose beds."

"Wait. You can't just start there. Which bedroom are we doing?"

"We're just going to get all the beds at once. Then we'll move on to chairs and so on." Benedict tapped the screen. "It's efficient."

Emma studied his face for signs that he was having her on. "You're joking, right?"

"Why would I be joking? Are you telling me there's another way to do this?"

"You aren't joking. What am I going to do with you?"

Benedict slid the mouse over to her side. "If you think there's a better way, you'd better enlighten me. Just make it quick, we have no time to waste."

Emma got out her phone, connected to his laptop, and transferred photos she'd taken of each room.

She found the tab that said *see this in your space* on the furniture shop's website and clicked. "I suggest we start with the bedrooms along the top and work through them one at a time. Any objections? No? Right. Let's get started."

Emma navigated around the shop's website with ease and knew exactly the kind of furniture she had in mind for each space. In less than five minutes she had a full-color mock-up of the bedroom at the far end of the corridor.

They worked through each room, figuring out which pieces of furniture to keep, which were ready to be retired, and what they needed to buy brand new.

"Why are you so familiar with this software?"

"Well, sometimes the brides that I work with end up feeling like they trust me so deeply that they ask me to decorate their wedding venue too. I don't always say yes, but I have been known to take it on and when I do, this type of software saves us both tears and heartache."

Emma opened up the next room, and they pieced it together in record time. Other than a disagreement on a green mat that Benedict swore would elevate the room, but Emma thought was simply hideous, their taste seemed pretty similar.

They covered it all, furniture, soft furnishings, bedding, and curtains. The bathrooms got towel rails, soap dishes, bathroom mats, toothbrush holders, and facecloth hooks. Once they'd gone through all the rooms, she opened it to check quantities, saved it as a pdf, and emailed it to the store.

"Right, that's that."

Benedict was quiet. Quiet enough to make Emma worry.

"Have I done something wrong? Was I too pushy? Because you said you need efficiency and that was the quickest way—"

He patted her arm and his fingers rested on her skin. "That was perfect. You're a ray of sunshine."

Chapter Twenty-Seven

EMMA AND BENEDICT WERE painting the walls side-by-side in the sunny room that Thomas had used as an art room.

Benedict twisted around with his brush waving in the air. "This room would make a great studio, don't you think?"

"You nearly painted my face. Be careful with that thing."

"Oops. I'll try harder next time."

Emma glared at him long enough to make him grin. "You're right though. Painting here would be most inspiring." She'd been thinking of Thomas, hoping he was getting on with his paintings. Being in this room doubled the number of thoughts that went his way. "Can I ask you something?"

"Sure."

"Why did you try to set me up with your brother?"

"I did not. What are you talking about?"

"Benedict. You very clearly did. That was such an obvious setup. You're insulting both of us if you think we wouldn't catch on."

He had the decency to look vaguely sheepish. "You'd be good for him. I thought it might be a good way to help him get over Dani. You know, the whole *there are other fish in the sea* story."

"Now you're calling me a fish. Aren't you just full of compliments?"

"Hmm." His eyebrows flicked upwards in a way that bordered on flirting.

Emma blushed to her roots and quickly became deeply interested in a spot on the wall that needed extra attention with a paintbrush.

"So what did you think?" Benedict was painting the wall, but she could feel the weight of his attention on her.

"Of your complimenting skills? For a handsome guy like you, they could do with some work."

"So you think I'm handsome. Hmm?" There it was again, that *tone*.

"Oh come on. You look in the mirror every day. What do you think?"

"What I think doesn't matter. What you do, however..." his voice trailed off.

Emma clicked her tongue in annoyance that wasn't a complete pretense. The effect he had on her was just too much to cope with. "You called *me* a fish. Well, I think you're *fishing* for compliments."

Benedict let out a genuine laugh and it made Emma's toes curl in delight.

"Seriously though, what did you think of Thomas? He's a great guy."

"I'm sure he is."

• • • ● • ● • • •

Emma, Thomas, and Dani were crammed into Dani's small flat, ready for their first intervention meeting.

"Guys, I know we're here to talk about this *intervention* or whatever it is, but I still want to know how you got back together again."

Thomas and Dani exchanged a look that left them both smiling.

"You tell, Dani. I'll take too long and we've only got Em for a short while."

"Okay, fine. Here it is from my perspective. So I never wanted to break up with Thomas and I really liked you, especially since you saved me from that awful speed dating night."

Thomas groaned. "My brother, man, he's got some really weird ideas, but I think speed dating was one of the worst."

Dani laughed. "So bad. Anyway, so seeing the two of you together really undid me. I couldn't even think straight. I didn't know what to think, but I felt like I'd been played twice. But Thomas coming running. Running! This boy doesn't run for anything." She shot him a look and her face softened. "Well, except me apparently. Anyway, he caught up and I could see that he was beside himself. The clincher was finding out that Benedict was behind the so-called dinner date."

Thomas let out a noise that almost sounded like a growl. "Emma, I told Dani how much you helped me to realize that I didn't want to lose her. It was you who helped me understand how I was feeling. Somehow around my brother, it just got all muddled. He argues so well. I couldn't answer him and he steamrolled me into something I didn't want. I know he's just trying to look after me, but in this case, he's wrong."

"His heart is good, though. There's just something going on that is breaking how he sees life." Dani spoke calmly.

Emma watched her words settle over Thomas and soften him. "You guys are so good together. I don't understand why Benedict can't see it."

Thomas waved at Dani's laptop. "Which is what we're going to try to figure out. His weird ideas have to come from somewhere."

Dani flexed her fingers. "That's enough chatting, we should start. Let's check social media. You're his brother, which platforms do you think he's active on?"

Thomas waved her off. "Don't ask me. We avoid each other as much as possible. I don't want him in my business any more than he already is and he certainly doesn't let me in his."

"We can work with that. Let's see." Dani clicked, typed in Benedict's name, hit enter, and waited.

Emma watched the two of them with their heads together, talking softly over Dani's laptop, and felt joy bubble inside at the rightness of it all. Sometimes things worked out, sometimes prayers were answered. Meddling big brothers, or not.

Dani rubbed her chin. "Okay, nothing there. Let's try this one."

Emma drew her legs up and felt her body relax. Dani's couch was comfortable and it had been a long time since she's just sat still without a list of things as tall as a house to get to.

Dani seemed more agitated with each click. Five minutes into her search, she sat bolt upright in shock. "This can't be right."

"What's going on? How bad is it?" Emma braced herself and sat up to resist that lure of the soft cushions. She wasn't prepared to admit it out loud, but Benedict had grown on her. She wasn't excited by the prospect of finding out something horrible about him.

"There's nothing online about this man. I mean *nothing*." Dani wasn't satisfied.

Thomas was scratching his chin as if that would help him remember. "He won a poetry competition when he was thirteen. Check the Poetry for Life page for teen winners, they should have them listed by year since the first year they ran it."

Dani typed, clicked, scrolled, and shook her head. "Look, there's a big blank for the year he would have won."

"I'll agree that it is weird, but I don't think it's criminal, right?" Emma wasn't following.

Thomas's lips were drawn in a tight line. "It isn't normal. I have a theory that there's something about everyone on the internet. If you search your name, you'll find something come up, right? The fact that there's a vacuum, looks like he's gone to great lengths to remove all traces of his existence from the internet. Why would he do that?"

Something about this was annoying Emma. "Guys, why are we doing this? If you're looking hard enough, you're going to find something suspicious. Do you know what I'm saying? What's the point? Also, why don't you just ask him? He may surprise you."

Thomas sighed. "Oh, I have. He clothes himself in mystery and dodges all my questions. There's more going on than what he's telling us. I'm worried, Em."

"I don't know. He seems to have his life together?" Emma frowned, "Apart from trying to break you two up and get me and Thomas together, that is." She grimaced. "Okay, that was bad. Maybe you guys are right."

Dani turned her laptop around on the coffee table and adjusted it so that Emma could all see. "Look, nothing. All the sneaking around, all the secrets. I don't know, Emma. It's very suspicious."

• • • • ● • ● ● • • •

Emma tried to put their meeting out of her mind. With the house deadline moved up, she'd been spending a lot of time with Benedict and she'd seen many other sides to the man. A guy who danced while painting a wall and who left a patch unpainted so as not to disturb her favorite little spider couldn't be secretly sinister, could he?

Despite her attempts, their conversation had planted seeds of doubt and she found herself on high alert for anything suspicious. She also got annoyed with herself every time she caught those thoughts in her head. *Ugh.*

She was adding the final touches to the main *en-suite* and she needed his opinion. They'd also need to start thinking of art for the walls. If Thomas wasn't so dead set on keeping his talent a secret from his brother, they could commission him. These two were *complicated.*

It was easy to find him, she just followed the sound of his voice through the house and it led to the kitchen. He was on the phone. Emma hung back, not wanting to interrupt.

He sounded agitated and she turned to quietly leave, but she couldn't help overhearing.

"I'm not happy about this development. I know what's going on here. You need to fix this. I don't care who you have to take out of the picture to get it done, just do what you need to do."

The edge to his voice sent a cold shiver through her. He turned, saw her, and ended the call.

"Sorry to interrupt. I need your opinion in the *en-suite* and we need to think about art for the walls."

"I meant to tell you, I have a plan for the walls. It involves dressing up though."

Chapter Twenty-Eight

"Benedict! Help!"

Benedict put down the paint tin and ran to where Emma stood at the base of the staircase watching a stream of water flowing down the stairs with gentle grace.

"There shouldn't be water coming down the stairs." Benedict watched the water flowing towards him for a full five seconds. It was only as it touched his shoe that he jumped into action to do something about it. "Grab towels from the cupboard in the hallway and try to stop the water from reaching the carpet in the main bedroom. Go!"

Emma sloshed off through the water and Benedict ran outside to turn off the mains. Everything around him moved in a slow-motion blur as he reached for the crank and threw his weight into it.

Only when the water was completely turned off, did life slam back into a normal speed. The crushing weight of the pressure he felt to get this all done on time hit him hard and a wave of something unfamiliar slid through him.

Hopelessness. They weren't going to be done on time, there was no way.

He didn't want to go back inside to see how much damage had been done. From where he stood he could see the rose garden. The pruned bushes no longer looked stubby and hacked, but he could see shoots of brand new fresh green growth sprouting everywhere. Emma had been right.

Time to face the setback. His feet felt heavy as he made his way back inside. Emma was on her hands and knees in the midst of a pile of soggy towels.

"I think we caught it in time." She looked up and her face changed as her eyes met his. She pushed herself off the floor, dried her hands on the back of her shorts, and came straight to him. She got right into his space, close enough that he heard her as she whispered, "it's going to be okay."

Another wave of hopelessness washed over him. "I don't know. I don't think we can meet this deadline."

Emma stood close enough that he felt the heat radiating from her skin. "It must be possible. We just need to call in some extra hands. Right?"

Benedict felt her hope bounce off him and he shook his head.

"It's going to work out." Emma threw her arms around him and hugged him. His body stiffened and he stood like a flagpole, resisting the urge to hug her back. He lasted a few seconds before his arms moved of their own accord and tucked her close.

All the pent-up stress he'd been carrying in his muscles seemed to evaporate in the face of her softness and he held on as a sailor clings to a mast in a storm.

• • • ● • ● • • •

Emma suddenly realized what she was doing and tried to pull away but Benedict's arms were tight bands around her that she didn't want to remove herself from. He sensed her shift and stepped back.

Benedict cleared his throat. "Sorry about that. I just don't know how we're going to get this right."

"Here's what I don't understand. Firstly, why is it suddenly so urgent? Secondly, you're rich, right?"

"Emma!"

"I'm just calling what I see. Money isn't a real option for you. So why don't you call in extra people? You could have fifty people onsite in an hour and they would flatten this in no time at all. So why don't you?"

Benedict shoved his hands in his pockets and squirmed under her questions. "I can't tell you that. Trust me when I say I've got my reasons and if I could tell you, you'd get it."

"So tell me." She met his eyes with a gaze that didn't waver.

"We should go mop upstairs."

Emma didn't budge. She shook her head slowly, deliberately. "Whatever you're getting up to, I'm involved now."

He took a slow step backward away from her, then another, then he spun around and bolted upstairs in a way that was so out of character, she burst out laughing.

• • • ● • ● • ● • • •

Benedict had paint splashed all down the front of his t-shirt and forearms. As the patch of clean white spread to hide more of the dirty cream paint underneath, he felt his insides hollow. There was too much to do and not enough time to do it all. This would be the first time he wouldn't have a house ready for a family placement. The thought of it made him feel quite ill.

He heard the tinkling of ice blocks in a glass before Emma popped around the corner carrying a tray with two tall glasses of orange juice.

She set it down on a sawed-off log and handed over a glass.

"This looks good, we're making progress."

Benedict slapped his leg so hard, his juice slopped over the edge of the glass. "I nearly forgot. There's a thing we need to go to tonight. Get yourself cleaned up and dressed."

Emma sipped her juice, not affected by the urgency in his voice. "I don't know that I'm up to going out. The last time I was this tired," she paused to think, "no, I've never been this tired. Shouldn't we stay here and push to finish?"

Benedict wiped his hands on his shirt, leaned toward her, and whispered, "Trust me, you want to go to this thing. It will help us finish."

Emma drained the last bit of juice from her glass. "You just pushed the right button. What must I wear?"

• • • • ● • ● • • •

An hour-and-a-bit later, they pulled up outside a badminton hall that had been transformed for an event of sorts, though there was no telling from outside what kind of event it was. Emma wore a deep emerald green shift dress with diamante spaghetti string straps that made her feel pretty and *chameleoned* between casual or formal depending on what setting she wore in.

Benedict wore a casual open-necked shirt and jeans and didn't look like he'd spent all day painting. He'd probably manage to look smart even if he dressed in a potato sack.

"I don't think you've been completely honest with me." Emma pseudo-glared at him, "There's no way this has anything to do with the house." Her heartbeat sped up briefly. Could it be that he just enjoyed her company? She snuck a glance at him, trying to figure out what was going on in his thoughts.

He smiled at her but didn't say anything, just held out his hand.

She hesitated, knowing the gravity of giving in to his unspoken request. In a breathless rush, she slid her hand into his and tried not to cling as her legs went wonky.

The transformation inside the hall sent Emma's senses into overdrive. Artwork lined the walls and filled the space, photographs that made her see life through different eyes.

"Okay, I get it. Artwork for the house."

Benedict was in pure hunting mode, he barely acknowledged her but scanned the canvasses as if he were a hungry lion and they were fresh buck about to bolt. It made Emma want to giggle.

She saw one that might work for the living room, an angled shot of parquet flooring with light flooding across it. It was both completely abstract and absolutely gorgeous at the same time.

Before she could point it out, an announcement was made for them to take their seats.

Renovating was hard work and Emma felt every minute of it in her tired body. She hadn't spent much time merely sitting around and doing nothing since starting work in the house. This felt so nice. The chair was soft and comfy, Benedict still held her hand and she leaned in closer to say thank you and he slipped an arm around her and she stayed there.

An old lady in a glittering jade-colored dress took the stage and somewhere between the verse and the chorus of a song about a moon and a river, Emma nodded off.

Chapter Twenty-Nine

EMMA HELD HER BREATH and clicked send. The message to Brenda was simple. *You girls paint, right? Would you be willing to take on a charity house painting job?*

She set her phone down as Benedict walked into the kitchen, he may not agree to her calling in the troops, but if anyone knew how to keep secrets, it was her rock painting girls. She'd break the news to him gently after he'd had his morning coffee.

He slid onto the barstool, looking more disheveled and undone than she'd ever seen him. It was a good few hours before sunrise and they were both up to get going on the house.

"Tea and toast?"

"Hmm." He rubbed his eyes and stretched. "I can't believe you fell asleep last night. You missed some good acts. The ballroom and Latin American dance formation team were especially good."

She put down a cup of steaming tea in front of him. "Why didn't you wake me?"

"I tried. Without causing a scene, the best I could do was hold you up so you didn't fall off the chair. You were properly gone."

"Did you pick out any pieces for the house at least?" She coughed to hide her embarrassment, handed him apricot jam-covered toast, and took a bite of her own.

"There were some good pieces, none of them felt right for this house. I'm not sure what we're going to do."

Emma shut her mouth and resisted the urge to brag about Thomas. He could deck out this house in a day. But she said nothing. It just wasn't the right time. The atmosphere between them this morning carried the residue sweetness of the night before and wrecking it by bringing up his brother just wasn't something she wanted to do.

Emma realized that she felt quite comfortable around Benedict, which was surprising given the rocky start to their friendship.

"Well, I have to say the only reason I fell asleep last night is because you're such a slave driver."

"Ha! Excuse me, Miss *I just want to paint one more wall before bed*. I think we all know who the slave driver is in this relationship."

Emma's nose lifted a fraction. "You said we need to get the house done, so I'm getting the house done. You should be proud, not mock me, you big chop."

Benedict laughed. "You are, as usual, quite right!"

Emma felt a window of opportunity to mention the rock girls and leaped in before her courage failed her. "Today is deadline day, right?"

"It is, but we're just going to do what we can and that will have to be good enough. It's ready for people to live in, just not finished by my usual standards."

Emma waited for a break to speak. "That's fine, but I wanted to check something with you."

A beeping noise went off in his pocket. Benedict pulled out his phone to check it and rubbed a hand through his hair. His mood shifted. "It will have to wait. I need to go." He was almost out the door and down the steps when he turned around, walked back into the kitchen, and hugged her.

He left with the strangest smile on his face, one that made her tummy flip.

• • • ● • ● • • •

He'd been gone about an hour when there was a knock on the door. She opened to find her rock ladies all kitted out in old clothes with spare rollers and paint trays in their hands.

Brenda stood at the front, looking as grumpy as ever. Emma knew now not to trust Brenda's face as an indication of her mood, it was just the way she looked. Behind her, all the other regulars were grinning happily as if all their suppressed excitement was leaking out their eyes as sparkles.

Some of the ladies had men with them, Emma could only assume their partners. Trailing at the rear was a group of young men who wore t-shirts that said 'I owe, therefore I work' with 'student debt' printed in slanty red writing below.

Dani was there too, but the look on her face was less excited and more puzzled.

"We're here. Where do you want us?" Brenda spoke in a monotone, with the slightest lift on the word *want*. Emma knew her well enough now to recognize that as her version of excitement. Close enough.

"You guys came." Emma felt relief wash through her, followed by a quick stab of worry. "Follow me, there's a lot to be done." It didn't take long to divide them up between the outstanding tasks until the only one left without a job was Dani.

"How good are you with a silicone gun?"

Dani shrugged. "I guess we're about to find out."

"Let's go finish off the bathrooms."

They'd been working together, applying a fresh application of new sealant to the bathtub when Dani cleared her throat.

"Emma, how did you get to be involved with this house if you don't mind me asking?"

It was a loaded question, Emma could tell by the way her heartbeat sped up. "Why does it matter?"

Dani frowned at the half-empty tube of silicone in her hands. "I just found out that this was the house Thomas grew up in. It is the Holmes family home."

That explained why she found Thomas on the porch the night they met at rock planting. Benedict was getting his old house ready to sell. Emma couldn't help wondering how Thomas would feel about that, surely he should have a say in it as well?

"I had no idea. I was hired to oversee renovations. That's as much as I know."

Dani went back to the gap between the edge of the backsplash tiling around the bath and the bathtub. The smell of silicone was strong in the small room and it made Emma's head a bit light.

Dani was standing in the bathtub, squashed up awkwardly against the tiles. Her arm muscles strained to get a fine line of silicone out. "Can I ask you a question?"

"Sure." *No* almost slipped out, but Emma caught it in time.

"Why are you sleeping in a tent in the middle of an indoor garden?"

Emma didn't know how to answer that. "It just feels better. I've got to be on-site, it was part of the terms for me living here. I don't feel completely at home staying in the bedrooms. The tent is my own space, I guess that has something to do with it. Also, it's like camping but without the weather."

"You must be quite ready to go back to your home." Dani threw out the comment, mere chit-chat. It stung.

"I have to find another home first." Emma bit her lip as it came out. She didn't need to make her problems, Dani's.

"Don't you have a place?"

Emma floundered, she didn't want to be talking about the sad state of her life. "I guess you could say... I'm between homes at the moment."

Dani swung around so fast, the string of silicone she'd placed so carefully pulled free and swung on the end of the silicone gun as if it had a bad head-cold and a runny nose. "Come stay by me."

"You're kind, but I—"

"Just until you find a new place."

"Thank you, Dani, I'll think about it. I hope I can find something a little more permanent."

Dani was trying to wipe off the excess silicone with toilet paper and making a mess. "Sure, Ems. I'd love to have you come to stay over." She frowned at the mess in her hands.

"Let me help you with that. After this house, I know my way around many things that I didn't before."

• • • ● • ● • • • •

By the end of the day, all the outstanding tasks on the house were complete and Benedict was still missing. Emma had hidden in the bathroom and scanned places to rent on the internet. Nothing. It didn't take long to send everyone off with hugs and thank you's. Dani had hugged her last.

"Just come stay by me. Even if it's just a day or two or even a month."

Emma had made noncommittal noises, secretly hoping another plan would present itself.

Alone in the house, she wandered through each room, pulling on the corner of a duvet to straighten out a wrinkle, making sure a mat was completely straight. Satisfied that it was all as perfect as they could get it in the shortened time, she took down her tent and rolled it up with quiet efficiency.

Packing her things was also quick and it only took about five trips to get everything to the car. Fitting into her small car was like an advanced game of *Tetris*, but she got it all in.

She faced the house one last time, not willing to identify the feelings that threatened to overwhelm her. Leaving this behind meant closing the door on an entire chapter.

Praying seemed appropriate so she turned her heart toward heaven and waited for words to come.

Nothing.

She managed a strangled, "Thank you for sending people to help today." But even that stung, so she whispered a quick amen and climbed into her car. Another search showed that there were still no apartments in her price range. Even if there had been, it was too late in the day to organize something anyway.

Dani would have to be it for a few days.

She couldn't help glancing in the mirror as she drove off. The house glowed in the moonlight, looking fresh and ready for whoever was meant to come and stay.

For all their conflict, part of her had enjoyed working alongside Benedict, even their daily clashes. She was going to miss him.

Not that she'd admit it to another living soul. No, no.

• • • • • • • • • • •

Benedict pulled up at the Sapphire rescue house at 1 a.m. exactly as arranged. He parked and waited, feeling the familiar adrenalin rush. He had the strangest feeling that he'd been followed and that made his skin crawl. But he kept a keen eye on the road behind him and didn't see anything to back up his suspicions.

The front door swung back and a small boy came out clutching his arm. The mom followed with a bag on her back. They two moved through the dark yard, inching their way closer to the car with infinite slowness. There was no moon to help them and they couldn't use lights. As they got closer to where Benedict sat, he could see things weren't right. The little guy's face was wet with tears and the mom was holding it together by a thread. Now that she was closer, he could see it wasn't a bag on her back, but rather a baby, swaddled and strapped tightly to her.

As they got to the car, he eased the door open and helped them inside. The little guy winced as Benedict helped him in, but he didn't cry. His mouth was a compressed tight line. The arm he held onto so tightly was broken and he sported a black eye.

Benedict felt pain shoot through him. He should have got them out sooner. It stung that he'd be taking them to an unfinished house, but in the light of what they were being subjected to, that was the least of their worries.

• • • • • • • • • • •

Dani had a bed set up for Emma in the lounge and Thomas was there to help carry in Emma's things. Both of them stood dressed head-to-toe in black.

"What's going on? Are you both into goth pajamas?"

Dani nodded sagely. "Intervention. Get your *sleuthiest* clothes on, we're leaving in half an hour."

"Where to?" Emma's heart sank. The thought of confronting Benedict was not high on her list of things she could cope with.

Thomas looked unhappy but resolute. "I saw a message from COR, whatever that is, informing him that he's on a mission tonight so we're going to follow him and find out what's going on."

"Guys, I'm not sure I want to know what's going. What if we find out that he's a criminal? Then you have to report your own brother or live with the guilt. I don't know which is worse."

Sadness crept through Thomas's face and settled into his shoulders as an unbearable weight. "I'm not exactly excited about this either. We have to do it though, for his sake."

Emma saw an echo in their eyes of exactly what she was feeling. The terrible pull. "Let me find my black clothes. I'll be quick."

Chapter Thirty

BENEDICT DROVE HIS THREE charges through the dark night with a growing burn in his chest. He'd called ahead and found a COR doctor on duty in a hospital close to the house. The boy would need his arm set and be checked for other injuries. The mom may be injured too. She sat in the back seat, cradling her baby and shivering.

He met her eyes in the mirror and she flinched and looked away. She wore guilt and shame as an unbearable burden.

"You've made the right choice. They'll be safe now."

There was that feeling again. He checked the rearview but nothing moved on the road behind him. Maybe this was all paranoia. Whatever it was, he didn't like it.

The mom was crying softly, a normal response in Benedict's experience. Some cried, others shut down. Years of trauma seemed to affect people in different ways.

Benedict thought of all the lives he'd had in this car over the years. So much pain and damage. He couldn't help thinking that different choices could have avoided messes like this.

This, right here, was why he didn't think relationships were to be taken lightly. He'd seen it all. So much pain, so much fall out for little people whose biggest stress should be feeling bored on holidays.

Not this.

Not ever this.

Committing to someone was a big deal. Each connection with a person brought something out of them. Attaching your life to someone who brought light out of you was good. The opposite was not.

• • • • ● • ● • • •

"Who is that woman? Do you guys know her?" Emma whispered even though they were parked so far away, the noise would never have carried to where Benedict was parked.

Emma's heart pounded with unanswered questions.

Thomas waited until the car was just out of sight before starting the engine to follow. "My question is, where is he taking them?"

Dani was swallowing her emotions hard. "The little boy..."

She never finished her sentence, she didn't have to. They were all feeling the weight of what they'd just seen.

They drove in silence, following Benedict's car through the dark countryside. Thomas hung back when they got too close and sped up when they lost sight of the car. Following him became trickier as they drove into the residential areas.

"Where is he taking them?" It was past 2 a.m. but the mystery had them all wide-awake and on edge.

Dani squinted at a street sign that flew past. "My guess would be the hospital. Oh yes, look where he's turning."

Emma sat in the back, torn between wallowing in how good it felt to see Thomas and Dani so happy together, and the sheer ugliness of not knowing what Benedict was involved in.

Benedict pulled into casualty and Thomas parked just outside on the street. It wouldn't do to confront the man here. He ushered the woman and her small charges inside.

They sat in silence, all staring at the hospital door until eventually, Emma blurted out, "Now what?"

• • • ● • ● • • •

Two long hours later, Benedict walked out with the little guy sleeping in his arms. The mom carried the baby and they all looked deeply weary. The boy didn't stir as Benedict tucked him into the car with his plaster-casted arm poking out like a stiff tree branch. The woman carried the infant close to her chest and seemed to have stopped shivering.

Benedict took a minute to scan the surroundings for suspicious signs or a car he recognized, but he saw nothing out of place and dismissed his state of high alert.

He drove them to the house with a heavy heart. It would be so good if the house were ready for them but even so, at least they'd be safe. Even if Benedict had to go finish it all off himself, he would do that.

Fifteen minutes later he pulled into the driveway. The garden was beautifully tended, it looked so good.

"Stay here while I unlock." He ran up the stairs and let himself into the house. As he stepped through the front door, he knew there'd been a miracle. The hallway floor was brightly polished and there were fresh flowers in the entrance hall. He took a quick jog through the place and wanted to pinch himself to make sure he was awake.

Her tent was missing from the terrarium. The indoor garden was fully restored, filled with flowers, ferns, and hundreds of other plants that he didn't recognize.

There was a note taped to the door from Emma.

B,
Invisible James is a wonderful gardener. An employee shuffle might be a good idea. Just a thought!
E

The house was not only finished being renovated, but Emma's touch was obvious. From the way she'd hung the towels hung in the bathroom, to fully stocked grocery cupboards and fresh linen on the beds.

He was not given to emotion, but this got him and he blinked back the sting in his eyes. He rushed downstairs and collected the little guy who was still fast asleep. The woman was wary but he smiled and led the way.

They had few clothes but there were clothing shop vouchers on the main bed.

"Would you feel more comfortable being in the same room?"

The main room had a camp cot set up and the lady got the baby settled in next to her. Benedict tucked the young boy in next to the mom.

He took the house keys and placed them in the mom's hands. "Here's your fresh start. I still need to come to clear out the cellar, but the rest of the house is yours. There's a security guard on duty around the clock. You have the organization's number, message if you need anything and there'll be someone to help."

She spoke for the first time since he'd rescued her. "I don't know how to thank you."

Benedict shook his head. "The best thanks that you can give me is to live free and happy and raise your two in safety. That is enough."

She swallowed hard and nodded once.

Benedict let himself out and did a quick trip around the property to make sure the security guard was at his post.

Satisfied that he'd done everything he could, he got into his car and felt a wave of weariness wash over him.

One last thing. He got out his phone and opened up messaging.

Chapter Thirty-One

3 A.M. AND EMMA couldn't sleep. Dani's living room couch was comfortable and she felt welcome. She'd been trying to sleep since they got back but her mind kept turning over what she'd seen tonight and all the feelings that had been stirred up.

The truth was in another world, if life were different and their situation less complicated, she could have fallen for Benedict without having to fight herself every step of the way.

The sting of seeing him with another woman made her think it was probably too late. If he was involved with the woman he'd fetched, why would he sneak around and hide a relationship? Maybe he'd got himself involved with a married woman.

She tried to pray but her words got muddled and it was all too exhausting.

What she needed was to find a new place, cut ties with these people and start over. It was probably worth getting a job with a steady income.

She took out her laptop and even that stung. Would she have to give it back? She wasn't going to think about that right now. With a deep breath, she purposefully shoved her feelings off to the side. They were just getting in the way.

Putting Benedict out of her thoughts too, she opened up an internet search and was scrolling through apartments when a message came through on her phone.

Benedict: Thank you

Seeing his name and those two simple words undid all her carefully layered composure. She blocked him, then tucked herself under the soft feather duvet and cried.

Benedict slept for three hours and woke up refreshed. His mind was clear and he was ready for the next challenge.

He opened up the COR relocation software to see who was next on the list and what they'd need. A mom with three girls, one teen, a pre-teen, and toddler. Like working through a puzzle, he scrolled through available houses.

Jesus, where do you want this family?

There was a nice double-story available, but it didn't feel right. He kept going. A few more caught his eye, but none of them *popped*.

This was going to take an extra special location. Wait.

There was one down the road from a gymnastics studio. He paused and prayed. "This one?"

As softly as a double heartbeat, he knew. They had their next project. The next thing on his list was to check if Emma would come on board again.

Working with her had been so easy. She was reliable, confidential, and the donors loved her. It was time to begin the COR onboarding process. Once she was in, he would be able to tell her everything and bring her up to speed.

He stopped his thoughts there and checked the time, 9 a.m. was a decent time to message someone. He typed out a quick message and hit send.

The message didn't deliver. How odd, maybe her phone was off.

• • • ● • ● • • •

Emma rearranged the plants on her window sill for the fifth time. The apartment she'd moved into was nice enough, but it just didn't feel right. The neighbors to the left of her fought constantly (and loudly) while the lady on the right was learning how to play the violin and she was, it would seem, deeply committed to the process.

Emma thrived in space with a good bit of silence and this apartment was exactly the opposite, an assault on her senses in every way.

Thomas and Dani's invitation paper had taken up some of her time for the first two weeks of being in her new place and they were all done. Six piles, bundled up in a yellow ribbon, the cards were a bittersweet reminder that life seldom worked out as planned. At least Thomas and Dani were back together, that was the most important thing.

She turned the blank cards over in her hands and the light caught the flecks of gold and the beautiful rough texture she loved so much. Handing them over to Thomas and Dani would mean she'd have to explain who she was. Not a big deal, but more confrontation that could go badly and she didn't want that. Maybe she'd mail them later.

Notification of an email came through from Benedict but she marked it spam, as she'd done with the ten others he'd sent, and didn't open it. He'd give up sooner or later.

She spent a good bit of time each day scouring the job adverts but hadn't found anything that was a good fit yet. Benedict's generous payment was enough to see her through for a few months as long as she was careful, but it wasn't in her nature to do nothing. She'd received another lump sum after the house was finished, which was unexpected and generous but then generosity that came from plenty didn't mean all that much.

Her phone beeped and her heart rate sped up. *Ugh.* How long would it take to stop associating messages with Benedict?

It wasn't from him but his younger brother.

Thomas: Emma, Dani and I are officially inviting you to the launch of the restaurant at the lodge. Below is the link to the electronic invitation. This is all thanks to you, I want you to come. PS – Benedict won't be there.

Chapter Thirty-Two

BENEDICT'S MORNING RUNS WERE getting longer and longer.

Emma was AWOL, Thomas slept at home and made supper every second night, but other than that he was out. Benedict knew that isolation was part of the deal for the work he did, but this felt ... horrible.

The jolt of his feet slapping on the hard surface of the road helped. It made sense, it was predictable. That worked for him right now. He pushed hard and his body gladly took the punishment.

He'd stopped trying to *fix* Thomas. The boy's attitude had changed in a way that Benedict couldn't put his finger on. Usually, Benedict knew exactly what buttons to press to get a reaction from his brother. Now? Thomas just chuckled at provocation. He side-stepped conflict and cheerfully did his own thing.

Whatever that was.

Frustration burned inside Benedict.

The new house was moving along, all on track. But it didn't have the spark of life that Emma brought. Maybe it was his imagination.

His thoughts tumbled through his head in an endless loop. Nothing ever resolved. It was like they were stuck on a giant Ferris wheel. Never touching down, just cycling endlessly.

His feet took him through a park he didn't usually run through but he followed without question.

Slap. Slap. Slap.

Wait.

There was something white tucked into the hollow roots of a tree. Curiosity got the better of him, even though he was not happy about breaking his stride.

He bent low, crouching low so that his thighs burned from the effort, and reached into the hollow. His fingers closed around the smooth surface of the white object—a stone—and he retrieved it.

Benedict stretched out his back and examined his find. Painted in exquisite lettering, he read words he knew well.

Now faith is the substance of things hoped for, the evidence of things not seen.

There was no reference, but he knew the verse well, Hebrews eleven, verse one. He sank to the ground and stopped running.

He stopped thinking and reasoning and scurrying.

Benedict grew quiet and listened.

A breeze rustled through his hair and he shivered.

What are You saying, Lord?

• • • • ● • ● • • •

Emma sat in the taxi fiddling with the shimmery black skirt of her only evening dress that she'd dug out for the occasion. She'd bought the thing off a sale shelf years back, but it was a quality garment and carried her safely through awards dinners, formals in college, and the odd date. It seemed to fit better now than it had before, even though the sharp angles of her body had softened of late.

She studied herself in the reflection of the taxi window trying to ignore the niggle in her spirit. She checked her bag. Yep, there they were, Dani and Thomas's invitation cards. She'd slipped them into her bag in case the right moment presented itself, then she'd hand them over.

She wasn't agitated about admitting to them both that she'd been their original invitation designer. Sure, it would mean answering a few awkward questions but they'd come such a long way in their friendship that she was confident they'd understand.

Why was she so antsy then?

It got so bad, she wriggled on the seat of the taxi. The truth was, she knew what was bothering her, she just didn't want to face it.

Benedict.

Benedict needed to be at tonight's launch. Acknowledging the fact brought a flood of warmth through her that had nothing to do with her standing with the man and everything to do with the passionate desire of Heaven to see two brothers reconciled.

He had to know who his little brother truly was. She owed it to them all.

"Excuse me," she patted on the driver's shoulder, "can we take a quick detour?" The closer they got to Benedict's home, the more terrified she became. What if he were home and cozying up with one of his lady friends?

Stop it, Emma. This is for Thomas.

Do it for Thomas.

• • • ● • ● • • •

Benedict was having a rare night off. Well, he was trying to. He wasn't very good at being off-duty. Remote in hand, he scrolled through channels on the T.V. hoping for something to distract his mind from its eternal loop.

He ignored the knock on his door, hoping whoever it was would get the hint that he didn't want any cookies, didn't need his roof repaired, and he most certainly didn't want to donate to any charity that required folks to go knock on doors to survive.

By the third heavy pounding, he stomped to the door more than mildly annoyed.

It was Emma. Dressed up and more beautiful than he remembered her to be. Maybe he had lost his mind. This level of hallucination was off the charts.

"Get some clothes on, you're coming with me." Evidently, this apparition spoke.

"Excuse me? You disappear without a word. Ignore my texts, calls, and emails. And now I must get dressed up and come with you?"

Emma tapped a long finger on her chin and nodded. "Yeah, that's about right." She breathed quick and deep, in and out. It deflated her a little. "Please Benedict. You need to see this."

Curiosity got the better of him. "Take a seat."

In true Benedict style, ten minutes was enough to get cleaned up and dressed up. He took his cues from Emma and went ultra-smooth in his classiest three-piece. His hands shook trying to get his cufflinks in and he tossed them back in the box in disgust.

Locking the house, he paid the taxi, sent it off and helped Emma into his car. He'd go with her but on his terms.

He took a moment to compose himself before climbing in next to her. "Right. Where are we going?"

Chapter Thirty-Three

BENEDICT HELD BACK ON all the questions he had lined up to fire at her. He shut down the clamoring emotions too. Fortunately, he'd had years to perfect the art of doing just that. His senses ran so heightened by the mystery that it felt like the hairs all down his arms were standing straight up.

He kept his tone light and asked, "Will we be eating?"

Emma's eyes dropped to her hands and he caught her quick nod.

"Good. I'm starving." Benedict felt his stomach rumble on cue.

"Take a left up ahead and find a parking spot. We're here." Emma was more subdued than he'd ever seen her.

"Can you at least give me some idea of what I'm walking into? Emma?"

The silence dragged on but he waited.

"Do you remember what you thought of the terrarium in the house?"

Benedict laughed. "I wanted to get rid of it, I didn't think there was any hope. But you? You saw it differently to me. You saw life. I was quite blown away by that." He couldn't look at her. The memories that flooded to the surface stung like hot darts.

"That's what I was hoping you would say." She shifted in her seat to face him, her eyes burning with a strange intensity. "Tonight is one of those. I see something you don't." She studied her hands, and continued, "I hope you can see through my eyes."

They climbed out of the car and he held his arm for her. Gratitude flooded through him as she took it. He patted her hand, so pale and delicate against the stark black fabric of his jacket.

She stared at him as if weighing him up. "Let's do this."

• • • • ● • ● • • •

Emma's felt sick. Why had she fetched him? Thomas hadn't invited him on purpose but of course, she had to meddle, didn't she? That's what she did. She meddled and got *involved*, poking her nose in others people's business whether they wanted it there or not.

Benedict was supposedly the meddler, but Emma was starting to think that she was worse.

Besides that, why did he have to smell so good? The memory of him had grown fuzzy over the weeks she hadn't seen him. But the drive here had nearly been the end of her.

Her fingers shook and he must have mistaken it for cold because he covered her hand. Warmth flooded through her and she resisted the urge to pull away and run.

He leaned close as they approached the tall glass doors and whispered, "A restaurant. I hope I'm not supposed to recognize this place, because I don't."

"It's new. Tonight is the launch."

The restaurant was Africa-themed and they'd gone all out to create an authentically wild feel. Enormous clay pots and a living forest of trees and plants created the sense of stepping inside but straight into nature. It was beautiful.

A discreet cameraman stepped out from behind a tall plant. "Do you mind if I take a photograph?"

Emma shot a quick look at Benedict and found him frowning at her. "I don't have any objections, do you?"

"I'd rather not."

The photographer stepped in closer for a good shot. "I was hoping you'd both say that. Get in closer, please. Let's get a good shot. A handsome couple like you two will make my camera skills look good."

Benedict folded his arms over this chest, waiting for the penny to drop.

"Oh wait. You said you *didn't* want a photo."

Benedict held out a hand, "Sorry about that. I'm just not a great candidate for photos."

The photographer sighed. "Well, that's a shame. I feel like we're all missing out on an opportunity. You two make the best-looking couple I've seen here tonight."

Benedict slipped an arm around Emma's shoulder and drew her inside the building before the man could get pushy. "Kudos to him for trying to do his job, I guess."

"Though he really should learn to listen."

"That would help him, yes." Benedict laughed and pain shot through Emma. She missed him, there was no denying it.

Stepping through the doors made panic rise, yet at the same time, a strange calm settle in its wake. "My eye is jumping from stress. Can you see it?"

Benedict stared at her, unblinking for a full thirty seconds. "Nah, you're good, I can't see anything." Benedict leaned close to whisper through his teeth, "If this is bothering you so much, we don't have to do it. We can just go home. I'll even make you tea."

"You don't even know why we're here."

"And that's only because *someone* won't tell me." He side-eyed her but she didn't take the bait.

Emma patted his arm and pointed up ahead with a strange look on her face. An entire section of the wall was taken up with a larger-than-life painting of an African sunset, complete with animals silhouetted against the blazing orangey-reds of the sky. It was subtly backlit and poured atmosphere into the small reception area.

Benedict followed where she was pointing. "Oh wow." He froze and took it all in. "Is that a print? Why does it make me feel things?"

"True art does that." Emma had seen the planning for this piece, Thomas had sent her his rough draft but she hadn't yet seen it in real life. It was altogether captivating.

"This is incredible. Who is the artist?"

"Do you want to see the others?"

Benedict nodded and allowed her to drag him along, still staring back at the entrance piece. The reception room led to a low ceilinged corridor, with skylights punctuating discreetly lit dark wooden panels, and lush greenery lining the walkway. The effect was much like walking through a secret forest path with the light of the moon casting dappled shadows on the stones beneath their feet.

The walls of the hallway were lined with art, nestled in amongst the greenery as if they were moments in the African bushveld captured for all time.

Benedict patted Emma's arm. "I'm glad we came. I'm still not sure why, especially since you've been M.I.A. for the last while, but this is worth it. This art is on another level."

Emma could tell his mind was working overtime because he'd drifted off into his own world.

"Em, imagine this. We commission this guy to paint for our houses. Art is powerful. Imagine filling our homes with pieces that help restore the people who live in them?" The grin slid off his face as he turned to her. "Oh, sorry. I just got excited. I didn't mean to drag you into all of it. I'm sure that one house was more than enough for you."

Emma blinked fast to stop the sting that preceded waterworks. "Let's go meet the artist, shall we? He'd love to hear your thoughts on his work."

"He's here? Yes! Lead on. Let's go." Benedict almost bounced in excitement.

The end of the hallway opened out into a bar area to the right, which served as a waiting area for patrons when the tables were all occupied. To the left lay the low-lit glittering dining hall which was filled with the quiet buzz of conversation and the clatter of plates and cutlery.

Emma peeped into the bar area and spotted Thomas easily. He had his arm around Dani and they were straightening a bold painting of a cheeky-looking zebra that graced the wall next to a glowing water fridge.

Benedict must have seen his brother because he hesitated, but Emma pulled him forward. "Benedict, meet the artist. Thomas Holmes."

• • • ● ● • ● ● • • •

Benedict covered his confusion by laughing. "Funny joke. What is this, Emma? Some weird intervention?"

Dani nearly choked on her sip of soda and Thomas stood blinking like an owl.

Emma hugged Thomas. "This is brilliant, I'm so proud of you." Then she hugged Dani too. "I have something for you two." She dug around in her bag and pulled out a carefully wrapped parcel of handmade invitation cards and handed them over.

"There's nothing printed on them now, but when you're ready, just let me know."

Thomas and Dani exchanged a puzzled look but then Thomas lit up. "So you're that Emma! It all makes sense now." He leaned close to Dani and pointed her way with his thumb, "She was hired to do our wedding invitations."

Dani's face lit up. "And now we're all friends. Look at that."

Benedict watched them all chatting. This was exactly what he tried to avoid. Why were they all so buddy-buddy? "Excuse me, what is going on here?"

Emma ignored him, focusing instead on Thomas. "I'm sorry I didn't ask first. It was a last-minute thing. He needs to know."

Thomas froze, his eyes slipping from Emma to Benedict and back again. A short lady in an extravagantly sequined mauve dress shuffled up and tapped him on the shoulder.

"Excuse me, young man. I believe these fabulous paintings are yours? You are the artist, right?"

As Thomas turned to her, his body language softened. "I am, indeed, Ma'am."

"Oh good. Well, I want to commission you to paint a series of jellyfish for our holiday home in Ballito. Are you available to do that?"

Thomas hesitated and the lady jumped in real quick.

"It will be well worth your time. I want five pieces and I'm prepared to pay handsomely for them. She pulled him closer to whisper in his ears and Emma watched his eyes widen. "I trust that will cover your needs? You are a very talented young man."

Thomas was nodding. "I would love to paint your jellyfish for you." He pulled a business card out of his pocket and handed it to the tiny woman.

"Great that's settled then. My assistant will be in touch with the details." She patted his cheek. "Your work sings, thank you for sharing your talent with the world and with me." With a dazzling smile that showed off the dimple in her left cheek, she turned away and shuffled off in between the other patrons.

Benedict looked more puzzled than before. He tapped the zebra. "So you painted this?"

"I did."

"And you have business cards and everything?"

"I do." Thomas smiled at his brother cautiously.

There was a platform set up in the corner of the room for live bands to set up and play. Instruments were all set up and ready. The restaurant owner took to the stage and blew into the mic to check if it was working. He was a small, compact man, with a body that buzzed with energy. He never stopped moving.

"I'd like to thank you all for coming. Tonight we celebrate the launch of a new venture. I want to acknowledge my team. I won't mention names as there are too many and the food will be cold by the time I've mentioned them all. We've all heard it said that it takes a village to raise a child, well I want to tell you that it takes a large army to launch a restaurant." He raised his glass as if he were presiding over a wedding. "Here's to my team in the trenches."

A ripple of laughter and applause flowed through the room. The owner paused until things had quietened down. "I do, however, want to highlight an exceptionally talented young man who has single-handedly created the ambiance we're all enjoying here tonight. Isn't it fabulous?"

With the flamboyance of someone used to holding the spotlight, he flung his arms wide to take it all in. "In record time, this gentleman has not only understood what I wanted but has surpassed all my desires. He's worked tirelessly to meet the deadline and have them all done for you today. Ladies and gentlemen, meet Thomas Holmes, the genius behind all these paintings. Without them, this space would be empty. "Thank you."

The man threw out the same flamboyant hand-wave and the whole room turned to look their way. Benedict stepped back to get out of the attention.

A round of cheering filled the space and a deep blush crept into Thomas's cheeks. He shifted shyly from foot to foot and grinned at the floor as if it were his best friend.

Benedict stood in the shadows, staring at his little brother, desperately trying to reframe how he saw him. His mind spun in the fastest circles. How had he not seen this?

Thomas looked happy, more than happy. The boy was beaming and fully confident. Dani had stepped away to give him his moment in the spotlight but he pulled her close, hugged her, and kissed the top of her head.

Emma stood off to one side, as he looked her way their eyes caught and held. He mouthed across the buzz all around them, *you have some explaining to do,* but her nose wrinkled and she shrugged.

The restaurant owner clapped his hands to get everyone's attention. "Without further ado, let's eat." He showed them to the door with an arm gesture an aerobics teacher would be proud of.

Benedict took Emma's hand and pulled her close enough to whisper, "You have some explaining to do."

She didn't take her hand back or pull away, but her response had a fierce edge to it, "Frankly? So do you."

Chapter Thirty-Four

EMMA STOOD IN THE garden of the house she'd helped renovate and faced the door to the cellar that had been a mystery for so long. Many feelings stirred inside of her. Being back at the house felt awkward and strange. It looked good and the rose bushes were thriving, but it wasn't for her, and being back here come with a crushing weight of what might have been.

Benedict came jogging around the corner and avoided making eye contact. They were far from comfortable around each other even though the launch had broken the period of silence between them.

Dinner had been delicious, but awkward enough to make Emma's skin crawl. They shared a table with strangers. Polite conversations and the restaurant's live entertainment offered little chance to talk about any of the unspoken things between them.

Between mains and dessert, he'd asked if she'd work on another house for him and she'd said no on account of all the secrets. He hadn't said another word right until they were walking out of the venue. Emma had no intention of letting him drive her home and had called a cab.

The cab had already pulled off when he ran after her and asked if she wanted to see the cellar.

Partly because she liked to solve mysteries, *thanks, curiosity*, but mostly because he'd run after her, she'd unblocked his number on her phone and allowed him to message her for the sake of making arrangements.

The entire week after seeing him again, all she needed to do was close her eyes and she'd picture him jogging towards her. He made her jittery inside and she couldn't wait to close the book on this awful chapter of *feeling things too deeply*.

Facing the door, he looked pretty grim himself and she wondered what terrible things waited inside.

"Sorry to make you wait, I had to let the occupants know we're here so they don't panic."

"You can just call her your girlfriend, Benedict. Unless you're married?" Emma flinched as another possibility dawned on her. "Maybe she's your mistress. You know what? It doesn't matter. Let's just get through this."

"What? Why would you say that?" Benedict was either completely clueless or a consummate liar because he looked genuinely shocked.

It was time for one of them to come clean. "We followed you. The night you fetched them. We saw it all. You're always sneaking off, it doesn't take much to put two and two together"

Benedict studied the wall for a long moment before responding. "Oh Emma, let's just say your math skills need work. There are other options that you're not considering but that's a conversation for another day. Hear me when I say, I am not in a relationship and I haven't been in a very long time." He checked to make sure she'd absorbed that important fact before moving on.

"Right now? Let's take a moment to talk about you guys stalking me. I suspected I was being followed, but I never thought it would be my own family. I don't know how I feel about that." His hands slid into his pockets and one eyebrow frowned a little more than the other.

Emma loved his eyebrows. "Thomas and Dani were worried about you."

"And you?"

"For a smart man, Benedict, you can be rather obtuse at times. Can we open this door now, please?"

"I think you were worried about me too." He grinned at her and before she could say another word, he moved right along, took a deep breath, inserted the key into the lock, and turned it. "You ready?"

Blood rushed past her ears. "Seriously though, just tell me one thing, was there a crime committed in this room?"

Benedict coughed or laughed, she couldn't tell. "Quite possibly, but you're going to have to be the judge of that."

The door swung open and Emma gingerly took the few steps down into the cellar and sneezed. Years of dust lay congregated in thick clumps around the room, undisturbed. It took a few moments for her eyes to adjust to the dark.

Benedict fiddled in the corner, flicked a switch and one wall lit up with cheap star lights. A hand-painted cardboard sign was taped to the wall below the stars proclaimed this to be *my cave*, with the words *stay out!* scrawled straight onto the plaster underneath in thick red marker. A makeshift couch took up most of the space along one wall, though it seemed to be made from old tires and a dusty blanket.

"This was your kingdom?"

Benedict nodded. "No, no, dear. Not my kingdom. My *man*cave."

Emma bit her lips not to smile. "Oh sorry. Mancave. I like it." She glanced around, taking in the old sci-fi movie posters up on the walls, the tattered rug on the floor, and could imagine a kid being thrilled to have their own space like this. Why the big mystery though? That was beyond her. "I don't get it, where's the body?"

"Body?" Benedict looked at her as if she had lost her mind.

"The big scary reason why I wasn't allowed in. What am I not seeing?"

A flick of his eyes sent her toward a rickety shelf that seemed to be a trophy shelf. Medals hung off hooks and certificates were taped to the walls with sticky tape. Some of them had fallen.

"Oh, nice. Your achievements." She tiptoed across the dusty floor, hoping not to create a mini dust storm with her feet. Benedict had developed an intense interest in the floor though his focus had nothing to do with the dust.

Emma reached up for a trophy and rubbed the label. "Endeavour." Not quite what she expected. Moving on to the certificates, all yellowed with age, one after the other, the same words kept cropping up. *Good attempt, hard work, persistence.* Not a single first in class or gold award in the lot.

Benedict leaned on the wall. He'd switched from the floor to examining his fingernail.

"Are you going to talk me through this, or do I just keep going?" asked Emma.

He shook his head and focused on the nail.

Emma kept going, waiting for the terrible thing to show itself. One corner of the room was covered in photocopies of pages of a book. She leaned in close and tilted her head to read the title. "Warrior: Awake!" In between the pages, he'd stuck up pictures of knights all dressed up in their armor.

Benedict was staring out the door as if wishing the floor would open up and swallow him whole.

"Did you read this book?"

"I took it out from the library and I renewed it three times but then I had to give it back. I was tempted to just keep it and say I'd lost it, but that didn't seem very noble. It also would have meant I could never show my face at the library again and that wouldn't have worked. I loved the library. The librarian seemed to have a soft spot for me. She made copies of all the pages I'd bookmarked and handed them over the next time I came to get books."

"So you were a reader. That's good. Not many young boys are." Underneath all the photocopied pages sat a small army of fluffy toys. Without really digging, she could see a dragon, a crocodile, and a whale. "No teddies?"

"Teddy bears are creepy."

"And a lime-green dinosaur isn't?"

Benedict walked over and picked up the dinosaur. He stuck it in her face and let out a low dinosaur growl. "Look at that face. There's nothing creepy about it."

Emma sneezed, laughed, and shoved the dino aside. "You're going to have to help me out here. I'm not seeing the scandalous reason you didn't want me to see what's in this room."

Benedict lowered himself onto the makeshift couch and patted the open space next to him. Curiosity got the best of her and she sat down gingerly expecting it to be uncomfortable, but it wasn't too bad and she felt her body relaxing. She shook herself back to her senses.

Benedict was now studying the lines on his hands as if they contained answers to all life's questions. They sat close enough that their shoulders touched. It felt like the time they'd spent in the lift, and the time she'd slept through a live performance on his shoulder.

"So, let me ask you this. After working on a house together, what do you know about me?"

Emma didn't have to think to answer. "I'm assuming you mean other than the fact that you are ridiculously secretive?" The smile she graced him with was pure cheek.

His sigh was enough of an answer.

"Fine. I'll be serious. You don't do anything half-effort. It has to be full-on or not at all."

"Exactly. What is this room full of?"

Emma saw it, exactly where he came from and why this room made his skin crawl. "Benedict—"

"You see it now, don't you? This is a shrine dedicated to noble mediocrity. I couldn't see it as a kid, but now it makes me cringe."

"What are you saying?"

"I'm saying that I aimed too low. I shouldn't have been proud of certificates for *trying*. That's so lame. I crossed the stage for those with my head held high. What kind of fool was I?"

"Stop being so rude to tiny you." Emma felt heat in her cheeks. "Just stop!"

"Excuse me?"

"Stop it! I don't see that at all." Her blood boiled at his closed-mindedness.

"What do you see?" The man sounded genuinely puzzled that anyone could have an opinion that was different from his.

"I see a little guy figuring out who he is. Testing the waters to find his strengths and weaknesses. Learning to follow where his strengths led, finding out what he's passionate about, and pursuing that. I see humility. I see the kind of gentleness that makes a strong guy safe to be around. I love this room. I love what it says about you."

• • • • ● • ● • • •

Benedict resisted the swell of feelings her words provoked. He needed time to reframe and rethink it all. It might be possible that she was right.

Emma's voice was gentle. "Can I ask you something?"

He didn't trust himself to speak, a nod would have to do.

"Are you upset that Thomas and Dani are back together?"

"Not at all." There was no hesitation in his response.

"Do you remember the first time we met?"

A smile crept over his face. "I helped you buy birdseed." He'd seen her on her tiptoes in the aisle and his heart had known. Known *what*, exactly, he couldn't say, but it had been clinched by the sunlight in her hair that had dazzled him as she left the shop. Little had he known just where this golden-haired woman was going to take him.

"No, silly! Not the birdseed, I didn't mean that. The yacht club. You were dead set against their relationship and yet I saw that it was right. I sometimes see things you don't. Correct?"

"You're right, I know. The terrarium was the same thing."

"I'm right about this room. I'm right about the little guy you were. You can stop fighting him and you can stop fighting your brother. He's going to be just fine."

Benedict shifted closer so that their arms touched and Emma didn't move away.

"All I ever wanted from Thomas was for him to love Dani so fiercely that he was prepared to stand up to me and declare it. I wanted him to know that it was right so completely that a doubting brother wouldn't put him off. Now? He's there."

"He is." Her voice was soft, almost dreamy.

Benedict spoke softly. "You made that happen."

"I don't see it like that." She pointed up. Not at the ceiling, but way beyond the heavens to where Inifinity lived.

Benedict laughed, Emma did too and it filled his soul. "I can't say I'm surprised. Let me hear it."

"Did I renovate this house?"

"Yes," Benedict answered confidently, but then hesitated. "But also, no."

"Exactly!"

Chapter Thirty-Five

EMMA LET BENEDICT DRIVE her home, but he turned down an unfamiliar street instead. "I think you missed the turn." She pointed back in the other direction.

"I want to show you something first." He glanced across at her, "If that's okay?"

"I'm quite worn out, I—" Emma had reached her Benedict-capacity for the day. Resisting her attraction to the man was exhausting.

"It won't take long." He slowed the car and added, "Please?"

He would take her home if she asked and that was enough. "Sure."

They drove in silence and Emma let the rhythm of the road lull her. So much in her life was uncertain and yet she felt safe, not just in the car with Benedict, but knowing that God was able to take her where He wanted her, and crash through any impossible things along the way.

"Ems, we're here." His voice was gentle. "If you look carefully at the wall on the left you'll see a pale logo etched into the paint."

Emma didn't at first but then it suddenly became clear. "Oh, there! I see it."

"Welcome to a City Of Refuge. Hold on." He pulled to a stop and the security guard ran out, saw it was him, and tipped his hat. "Go right on in, Mr. Holmes."

"Was the logo made up of the letters c, o, and r? What's a city of refuge?"

Benedict drove on through a neatly kept suburb that felt peaceful and safe. "COR is a secretive organization that rescues families stuck in abusive relationships. We mark out territories, make them safe and prepare homes for those who need a fresh start. Our aim is to keep life as normal as possible for the survivors while keeping those that would harm them out. We've got nine COR villages established and are working on our tenth. All staff members are carefully screened. We have a selection of professions on board too, doctors, lawyers, and psychologists who we can call on if our survivors need help. It's not a faultless system, but we're working on perfecting it all the time and it's better than nothing."

Emma watched him speak and understanding dawned. "Your secrets are to keep these people safe?"

Benedict said nothing, but the smile on his face confirmed that she'd nailed it. He pulled into a parking spot facing the ocean. The sun sparkled on the restless waves.

"You became the cleaner at the pool. You jump in and rescue when nobody else notices someone is drowning. I think tiny Benedict would stick a picture of you on his wall."

"I think he would." Benedict's serious face cracked a smile.

Emma felt like seaweed clinging to a rock, pulled this way and that as the tides shifted. "Why can you tell me this now but not before? What's changed?" So much trouble could have been saved if he'd spoken up long ago.

"Well, you've proved that you can keep secrets." Benedict looked mildly put out by this fact. "Thomas told me he'd been using a room in the house as a studio. I had no idea and you never even dropped a hint. Considering that I'm a bit of a bloodhound for cover-ups, that's impressive. It hurt my feelings," he cleared his throat, "but it's impressive."

"So I can lie successfully. Great. Maybe I should put that on my resume."

"There's more to it than that of course." He stared at the ocean. "You're a hard worker, oh my soul, you're a hard worker. Those sleepless nights." Benedict sighed at the memory. "But that's not all. I mean, you have an eye for style that outstrips mine, but even that isn't what qualifies you." He shifted in the seat to face her. "You love God and He loves people through you. You *let Him* love people through you. That's rare and precious, Ems."

Emma weighed his words and they resonated. He was right. "What now?"

"So the big question is, now that you know all the secrets..."

Emma held her breath, too scared to hope...

"Will you come work for COR?" He spoke fast as if expecting rejection. "Think about before you say no. I've already got Thomas and Dani onboard. She's going to be part of the counseling team and Thomas will do what he does best. We'd make a great team together."

Her eyes stung. He could have asked her one of two things and he'd asked the one she didn't want to hear. "This sea-glare and salty air must be getting to me." She sniffed loud trying to mask her disappointment. "I'll think about it and let you know."

She was already planning where she could move to just to get away from him. Being emotional seaweed wasn't something she'd recommend as a fun time.

Benedict sat up and dug in his pocket. "I nearly forgot. This is for you." He pulled a slightly squashed piece of handmade paper out of his pocket. He straightened it out on his knee before handing it over. "You'll recognize most of this."

Emma took the invitation from him and grew quiet. She ran her fingers across the rough surface with the rose petals and gold flakes. "This is one that Dani made, I remember thinking how well she managed to balance the elements."

The surface was covered in a beautiful flowing script in gold ink which Emma had to blink a few times to read. "And Thomas wrote these by hand?"

Benedict nodded.

"They're getting married and I'm invited." Full-circle-faith. She shut her eyes and stopped trying to keep it all together.

• • • • ● • ● • • •

Benedict had tried to read Emma throughout the trip to the COR. He had so much he wanted to say, but he couldn't tell if she felt the same way he did. For someone so good at reading people, this situation was unacceptable and threw him completely.

As the day had dragged on, Emma had grown quieter and more withdrawn. By the end of the day, he'd dropped her at home with so many things still unsaid. With his confidence trashed, he dropped her off with a wave. No hug, no deep conversation, just a fake-cheerful *see you soon* and then he drove and mentally beat himself up for the rest of the night.

• • • • ● • ● • • •

Emma was trying to seal up the last of her boxes but the tape got all snarled up and stuck to her fingers more than the box. How ironic it was that this one was full of Paper List things. Her little wedding card endeavor was at an end and she was moving on. She'd applied for a couple of jobs and had a game lodge on the other side of the country contact her to take on an administrative position.

The thought of a change sounded so appealing, Emma didn't mind what job she had to do to make it happen. Even if it destroyed her soul.

Her doorbell rang and she assumed the movers were here for her things. She opened the door with one hand still all tied up in sticky tape to find Thomas and Dani.

Dani took one look at her, plucked the sticky tape off her fingers, and ushered her out the door. "We've come to fetch you, we're having a wedding meeting and we'd like you to be involved."

Emma flexed her sticky fingers, relieved to find they still worked. "What do you mean by *involved*?"

Thomas watched as she dumped her keys into her handbag and pulled the door shut behind her.

Dani smiled, looking a little relieved. "Honestly, I thought you'd fight us. Thank you for not."

Emma got into the back seat of the car to find half the seat taken up. Benedict was already strapped in and he gave her a resigned wave as she sat down.

"Er, guys? What's going on here?" Thomas shut the door behind her and the door locks clicked down.

Benedict rolled his eyes, "It's an intervention apparently."

"Another one?" Emma couldn't believe what she was hearing. "Are you in on this?"

Benedict shook his head. "They told me we were having a wedding meeting."

Thomas pulled off into the traffic. Both he and Dani looked ridiculously happy. The drive was too short to become awkward and they stopped at a local beach.

Thomas yelled, "Everybody out!" in a particularly dad-like voice.

• • • ● ● • ● ● • •

Benedict sighed but did as he was told and Emma followed his lead.

Thomas and Dani led them to a secluded cove where a beautifully laid-out picnic waited for them.

Dani nudged Thomas to speak and he kissed her cheek before turning to Benedict and Emma and motioning for them to sit on the tartan picnic blanket.

"Today would have been our wedding day." He shook his head as Benedict tried to speak. "We're grateful for what you did, Benedict. You were right, I wasn't ready. I had to almost lose the best thing that's ever happened to me to find the fire in my belly. Thank you."

He hugged Dani and turned to Emma. "Emma, you heard Heaven's whisper that we were right for each other. You didn't doubt or give up on us. The clincher was getting those invitations from you made was a sign we'd both prayed for. You were right too."

Dani spoke up, "So we feel that on this, er, *not-so-special* day, it's only fitting that we give you two a chance to see what we're seeing. Because it's pretty obvious, hey Thom?"

Thomas nodded. "So obvious. But there are rules. Rule one, you're not allowed to leave that blanket until you've said all the things you haven't yet said to each other. Rule two, you're not allowed to talk about things you've already spoken about."

Benedict looked across at Emma but he couldn't read the expression on her face.

Dani rocked back and forth with a cheeky little smile until Thomas grabbed her hand, "Come on, pudding, let's leave these two to get on with it."

Dani waved and let Thomas drag her away, though she kept throwing looks back as they walked off as if to see how the two of them were getting on.

Benedict waved them off and Dani laughed.

So these two had been plotting and scheming, but their magnificent plan dovetailed with his perfectly. He'd overheard Thomas on the phone to Dani planning this outing and had roped Invisible James in to do some secret preparation of his own.

A setup like this, handed to him on a plate? There was no guarantee that it would work out, but he had to try.

He'd never forgive himself if he didn't.

• • • • ● • ● • • •

Emma faced Benedict and the familiar wash of delicious turmoil churned inside. "This is unexpected."

He studied her with a softness to his expression that was new. "I didn't realize how bossy the two of them are. So, according to their rules, I can ask you if you've decided to work for me because we haven't discussed that since the other day."

Emma didn't want to face him when she delivered the news. She wanted to email him. Or text him. Or send him a note tied to the leg of a carrier pigeon. She was saved from answering by his hand on hers.

"Before you answer, I need to come clean. I haven't been entirely honest with you."

She barely flinched. "Oh? There's more? Big surprise."

"Are you being cheeky with me?" He wiggled a finger in her face but moved right along. "Your business, The Paper List. I have a proposal." He waited for her forehead to crease into a puzzled frown before he carried on.

"Within each City Of Refuge, we try to create opportunities for people to earn. I'd like you to train people to do what you do and create businesses from it. The paper you make can be used for many different things, it doesn't have to be limited to invitations. So instead of shutting it down, I'd love to see it grow and help people. Don't answer now. Think about it."

He stood up and stretched on his toes to check on Thomas and Dani. "I think we're safe, come."

"You want to break the rules?"

"Yes, come quickly before they're back." He scooped up the blanket, hung it around his neck like a towel, and reached for her hand.

Benedict was too excited for her to resist him. Who knew what he was up to this time?

He led the way down the beach in the opposite direction to Dani and Thomas. Emma followed, feeling the heat of the soft, white sand between her toes. The waves were lazy today, rippling in without much fuss and surrendering to the pull of the tide as they rolled back again.

Benedict whistled as they strolled along, then he halted and kicked up sand.

"What are you doing? This isn't coming clean. What's going on?"

Benedict looked red in the face though it may have just been from the sun. "What's going on? It's about to get really sappy on this beach. Brace yourself."

His eye line dropped to the ground and she spotted a rock at his feet, a very familiar-looking rock.

She picked it up as if she'd found an old friend. It was her faith verse from Hebrews, with the letters F, A, I, T, and H painted in bold across the top and the verse painted in full on the underside.

"I painted this and planted it! You found it?"

Benedict whipped a bag out of his pocket and held it out for her to place the rock in. "I did. I didn't know you painted it though. I found it and thought you'd like it." He shook his head in wonder. "Isn't that a weird coincidence?"

"When I planted it, I prayed that whoever needed it, would find it. So maybe you needed it." These coincidences didn't shock her half as much as they used to. "Listen, I hope that rock wasn't meant to be the sappy thing because if it is ... Let's just say, I'm expecting high levels of sap. You'd better not disappoint me."

"Oh, it's still coming. Believe me." He grimaced and walked a few steps further where they found another rock, larger than the first, one Emma had never seen before.

He tapped it with a sandy toe. "You definitely didn't paint this one."

The top was covered in a beautifully painted sun. Emma ran her fingers over the smooth surface. "Is this Thomas's work?"

Benedict shook his head and patted his chest.

"You can paint? Why have you never told me?" Emma turned the rock over. It was covered in fine writing.

Falling ...
... I blame the birdseed. That was the start of the fall. I didn't realize how hard or how fast the fall would be. I had to join your line and when you left the shop, I watched the sunlight dance in your hair and I knew you were the one I wanted.

Emma read the words and her heart pounded. Birdseed. The atmosphere shifted and she felt heat in her cheeks. Birdseed took her way back to their first meeting by chance in the grocery store. She held onto the rock and let him lead her to the next one. This had a simple painting of water, sky, and a yacht.

He took the sunshine rock, leaned close, and whispered, "Sap incoming."

Emma picked it up and held it in her hands. She loved the contrast of the colors, it reminded her of one of her favorite paint swatches.

Argue ...
... You argued with me. In your ripped jeans, no match for my suit, but you didn't care. I couldn't intimidate you. Your arguments engaged my mind, but it was your passion that snagged my soul.
This, dear Em, is what I fought against.

Benedict pulled his best I-told-you-so face and skip-hopped to the next rock, which he presented with a flourish. The top of this rock was covered in a night scene of a house lit up from the inside, blazing light through the darkness. It warmed her palms as she turned it over.

Ideas ...
... And then the house. Your annoyingly perfect ideas. Your stubborn refusal to let me intimidate you. How, dear Em, did that make the slide quicker? Explain, please.

Emma dare not speak over the lump in her throat. She followed Benedict to the next rock. Covered in plants and flowers, she guessed the word and smiled when she turned it over to see she was right.

Terrarium...
... The mess in the middle is all I saw. You saw more and you brought it back to life.
Tiny me and the cellar, the mess in the middle. You saw more and you've brought me back to life.

Emma didn't look at the man, she couldn't trust herself. He walked ahead to the last rock and stood, staring out at the ocean. He'd painted paint swatches onto the rock. One was made up of monochrome blocks named *gloomy doom*, *not-breathing blue*, and *shadowy heartbreak*. The one next to it was almost blinding the colors were so bright. *She-loves-me-too lilac, happy hopeful heart* (which was a shade of orange), and *from now on*, a bright, happy, shade of blue.

Here ...
... Here, now. You and me.
From here into always.
What do you think?

She read the words, but they blurred and her mind tripped up over a tumbleweed of hope and don't-dare-hope.

He stood a few steps away, hands clutched behind his back, "Faith. "You see, Em, you are the substance of everything I've ever hoped for. You are evidence of the goodness of God to me. It's that simple and that complicated."

Emma turned the rock over, trying on the feeling of *being loved* as one would try a coat in a shop. Maybe there was one in her size after all.

Benedict stepped in close, his hands closed around hers and the rock as he whispered, "You and me, Em. What do you think?"

"Well, we've never talked about this before, so it's not breaking *that* rule. We're not on the picnic blanket though, so that's a problem..."

Benedict took the rock, put it in the bag, and dropped the whole bag in the sand. He stepped back, arms at his sides and a cheeky sparkle in his eye. "That's why I brought it along."

He pulled the blanket off his neck, spread it out on the sand, and stepped onto it as if they'd never sneakily escaped. "Come over here," his foot tapped the blanket, "it wouldn't do to break rules, now would it?"

He held his hands out, vulnerable, open.

"Were you in on this intervention all along?"

"I overheard their plans, and made some of my own with a little help from our guard-turned-gardener, James." He was still waiting.

Emma stood frozen, her mind and emotions spinning wildly to recalibrate. All the unspoken things had been said. They tumbled through her buffeting feelings into alignment with reality. Everything she'd hoped for stood waiting in front of her.

As light as a downy feather, she stepped onto the blanket, into his arms and her heart found home.

Chapter Thirty-Six

"Well, that wedding was perfect." Emma snuggled her tired body into the passenger seat while Benedict drove away from the venue where they'd spent a full day celebrating Thomas and Dani's marriage. "It's probably a weird thing to say because it also involved some ripping and not the sort that I usually do for weddings."

Benedict reached over to squeeze her hand while they waited at a traffic light "I don't know that I'd call a wedding where the bridesmaid steps on the bride's dress and rips it as they walk down the aisle, perfect, but it didn't seem to throw Dani off at all."

"Exactly. Even when the waiter tripped on Aunt Gladys's yorky and pushed the cake over. Even that didn't ruin the day. Who brings their dog to a wedding?"

Benedict laughed, "Aunt Gladys! Apparently he was her plus one." He steered the car onto an unfamiliar road.

"Thomas and Dani looked happy, though. Didn't they?"

"So happy, it was almost embarrassing."

Emma play-smacked his leg. "You looked pretty chuffed yourself, so don't go ragging them." She sat up and looked out the window. "Where are we going?"

"I want to show you a house."

"Are you kidding? No, Benedict, come on. I'm so tired. Can't work wait for Monday? I know the list is long at the moment, but—"

"We're here."

Emma groaned and weighed up how much energy it would take to argue with the man, compared to how much she'd use by humoring him. In the end, it took too much energy to even it work out, so she slid out of the car and leaned on him to keep herself upright.

She never wore heels other than weddings and her feet were lecturing her from down below. "Do we really have to do this now?"

He kissed her forehead. "Come on."

The pathway that led from the driveway took them down steps and through a garden lush with ferns, leafy *Monstera*, and a creeping Jasmine that filled the afternoon air with its scent.

Emma forgot about her aching feet as Benedict walked her through a house that ticked every item on her *one day when I have a house* list.

He slid the giant patio doors back to open the living room to a view over the ocean. The setting sun lit the water in sparkling shades of orange and blue.

Emma stood at the rail with a full heart but a growing question in her head. Benedict joined her and breathed the fresh sea air in deeply.

"I think you may have lost it a bit. Why would we need to fix this up? It's perfect."

Benedict was tickled pink, she could see it in the pull of his mouth when he tried to suppress a smile. "So you like this one?"

"It's absolutely perfect, but I wouldn't want to work on it because changing anything would be a crime."

"I see." He rubbed his chin as he did when he thought deep things.

"Don't get me wrong, I'd happily move in here to renovate. I just don't know what I'd reno—"

"Would you move in here for this?" He took her hand and slipped something small and cold into her palm.

"Are you bribing me now, Mr. Holmes?" she teased with fake coyness.

His eyes though, locked onto hers with an intensity that made breathing hard. "It depends. How do you feel about becoming Mrs. Holmes?"

Emma's hand flicked open so fast, a ring went flying. They both scrambled for it, collided, slipped on the tiles, and went down like bowling pins in a strike. They lay there, dazed, in a tangle of arms and legs before Benedict raised a fist.

"Got it."

He was so close, Emma felt his heart rate speed up as he leaned towards her.

"Emma Redwood, I would like to promote you from chief house renovator," he held up the ring and the afternoon sun sparkled through the diamond, "to my wife. Will you marry me and then come live in this house that doesn't need a single thing fixed up?"

Warmth and love rushed through Emma in a flood.

"Hold on." She fiddled in her bag, managed to avoid elbowing him in the face by a hair, and found a paint swatch that she'd been saving for an occasion just like this. It was all tattered around the edges and a bit crumpled, but she handed it over to Benedict.

The three blocks declared:

Don't mind if I do (cherry pink)

Of course, I'll marry you (lemon yellow)

Please kiss me (pale lime green)

A smile of pure joy lit Benedict's face but only for a second because you can't grin like a loon and kiss your brand new fiancée at the same time.

Sometimes you have to choose.

Thank You

Thank you for reading The Paper List, I hope you enjoyed it! The great love between Benedict and Emma played out over 36 chapters, but the love story between you and God? That will last your lifetime and beyond into eternity. He's rather smitten with you!
(It might not feel like it all the time, but ... it's true.)

If you haven't read The Cake List, or The Never List yet, you can go right ahead and catch up now, as the stories are stand-alones, even though the worlds touch.

I'd love you to leave a review on Amazon, Goodreads, or Bookbub. I may even break out in a little happy dance.
Reviews help other readers decide if a book is the type of reading matter they like.

For You

Claim your free quick-read when you sign up for my newsletter at www.diannejwilson.com.

Samantha loves Max. He's finally noticed her and invited her to a ball. But what's a jeans-and-t-shirt girl with zero budget going to do when fairy godmothers don't exist?
The Hairy Godfather
Because sometimes love needs a little help.

About

Dianne J. Wilson writes across genres including women's fiction, humor, romantic suspense, and the odd stab at YA fantasy. Weaving Invisible into words, she explores spiritual truth woven through ordinary life with equal dashes of breathless adventure and tongue-in-cheek humor, all soaked in God's Grace.

Her early books were written in stolen moments, usually in the back seat of her tiny car. Then she graduated to a couch or the bed. Now, at last, she has a desk of her own that she occasionally has to share with a cat or two.

Her home is in Makhanda, a South African university town, where she lives with her hubby and three daughters who all take turns at being home.

Her love-language is tea and taking long drives to listen to new songs with her girls. When she's not writing, you can find her feeding all the hungry people and cats in her house who gaze at her expectantly around mealtimes.

Please visit Dianne's website for more of her books: www.diannejwilson.com

Find Dianne on:

Amazon

BookBub

Instagram

Facebook

Goodreads

Also by Dianne J. Wilson

Contemporary romance and mystery that is feel-good, faith-filled and funny

THE LIST BOOKS

The Cake List
The Never List
The Paper List

RIVER VALLEY ROMANCE

Inheriting Ubomi
Running Ubomi
Raising Ubomi (releasing 2023)

Romance on the run ... suspense, mystery and faith

SUNSHINE COAST MYSTERIES

Shackles
Undertow (releasing 2023)

STAND ALONE

Finding Mia

What if we could see into the spiritual realm?

THE SPIRIT WALKER TRILOGY

Affinity
Resonance
Cadence

Rom-com quick reads

MEETING UP WITH LOVE
(10 Author Collaboration)

Meeting Up With The Architect

Devotionals for when you need a hug from Heaven

When God's Dreams Meet Your Reality
(previously released as 'Messy Life')

In All Things - 13 Weeks of Devotions from Africa
(11 Author Collaboration)

230 DIANNE J. WILSON

Purchase Link To All Titles